FOR LOVE OF AN ISLAND

Staff Nurse Tessa Ferguson, engaged to charismatic cardiac surgeon Jerry Talbot, looks set to enjoy a wonderful future until she unexpectedly inherits a remote Caribbean Island. Jerry wants her to sell it to finance his own ambitions, but when Tessa visits St Christos and meets attractive Alex Ross, she has a change of heart — and through the danger that follows, Tessa must decide where love and loyalties truly lie.

Books by Joyce Johnson
in the Linford Romance Library:

JOYCE JOHNSON

FOR LOVE OF AN ISLAND

Complete and Unabridged

LINFORD
Leicester

First published in Great Britain in 2003

First Linford Edition
published 2004

British Library CIP Data

Johnson, Joyce, *1931* –
    For love of an island.—Large print ed.—
Linford romance library
    1. Love stories
    2. Large type books
    I. Title
    813.5′4 [F]

ISBN 1–84395–308–0

Published by
F. A. Thorpe (Publishing)
Anstey, Leicestershire

Set by Words & Graphics Ltd.
Anstey, Leicestershire
Printed and bound in Great Britain by
T. J. International Ltd., Padstow, Cornwall

This book is printed on acid-free paper

1

The maternity ward of St Judes buzzed with speculation. Fiction outstripped fact and rumours multiplied as nurses competed to add their own bit of gossip about the latest hospital romance. Sister Bedford appeared the most authoritative.

'At the consultants' dinner last night — Dr Green was there, he phoned me late last night and . . . '

'But he told me this morning Mr Talbot proposed in the moonlight by the Thames. Oh, so romantic,' Emma Bailey, the youngest nursing recruit, sighed enviously.

'He's teasing you. How could he have known that?'

'No-one's ever seen them together.'

'She's late. We'd best get on.'

Sister Bedford glanced at the ward clock.

'She's never late, and here she is. After last night she's entitled to . . . '

Emma tailed off as Tessa Ferguson's tall figure moved swiftly towards the nurses' station.

'Sister, I'm so sorry but the traffic was really dire.'

Tessa tucked a strand of blonde hair under her cap and smoothed her uniform. Sunlight streaming through a window struck sparks from her finger and someone caught her left hand and held it out for general admiration.

'A gorgeous ring!'

'Nobody guessed.'

'You're a sly pair.'

'When's the wedding?'

'He's a great catch!'

One or two of the older nurses eyed Tessa doubtfully, wondering what the charismatic consultant, Jerry Talbot, saw in Staff Nurse Ferguson. But while their eyes doubted, their mouths smiled and added congratulations with the rest. Sister called her staff to order.

'Best wishes, Tessa, but there are

patients to look after. Two new patients overnight to chart and monitor. Make a start and maybe we can meet up in the pub later to hear the romantic details.'

'Of course, but it'll have to be later in the week. Mother's due home tonight and so far she doesn't know about the engagement.'

Sister's eyebrows rose.

'I bet she does. Not much gets past your mother in this hospital, or St James's. Surely she at least knew you were seeing Jerry.'

'She's been very busy and . . . well, we didn't . . . Jerry didn't want . . . '

'No need to explain. I expect she'll be delighted anyway. Now, let's have a look at Mrs Jones. Her blood pressure is a bit high.'

The ward routine slipped effortlessly back into gear. Tessa was glad to be busy. Although paediatric nursing was her career choice she was enjoying her spell on the maternity unit. This was where life started and, of course, this was Jerry's field of work. She pushed

aside thoughts of Jerry as she concen-
trated on the mother-to-be.

'Not long now. A boy, isn't it?' she
asked the girl.

The girl nodded.

'Can't be too soon. He's already ten
days overdue. Hey, did we hear right?
Are you really engaged to Mr Talbot?'

'Yes, yes, I am.'

'You don't seem very excited. I'd be
delirious if I were engaged to him. He's
so attractive.'

'I am excited but, well, it was a bit
sudden, like a . . . '

She searched for the right word.

'Fairytale,' the girl supplied, as Tessa
moved away.

She had met Jerry Talbot only five
weeks ago at one of her mother's
work-cum-social dinners and she'd
been more than a little in awe of him.
His rise from houseman to consultant
had been meteoric and now at
thirty-two he exuded competence and
confidence and was assured of a
bright future.

She and her friend, Helen, had tagged along at the dinner party to oil the domestic wheels of the evening. Jerry fitted easily into Margaret's high-powered circle of academics and medical professors and he paid little attention to either Tessa or Helen, or so it had seemed to her at the time!

She moved on to her next patient.

Tessa was very late leaving the hospital that evening. Her mother, a professor in general medicine, would be home from her seminar in Milan and would expect her daughter to be there to hear all the latest European medical gossip. Tessa took the luxury of a taxi home and ran up the steps of their home. The front door was opened before she could insert her key.

'Hi, Tessa. You're late but your mother's not home yet. Plane's delayed and she's calling in at Martin's first. May have dinner there, so don't wait.'

Message delivered, Molly Woods, housekeeper to the Fergusons ever since Tessa could remember, pulled her into the hall.

'And you look exhausted. Go and have a bath. As it's just you, we'll eat together in the kitchen. Casserole and dumplings.'

She took Tessa's coat and pursed her lips.

'Mebbe a dram of whisky and hot water! All that excitement last night's taken it out of you. He telephoned half an hour ago. There's a mammoth bouquet in the garden room and he'll call you later from Brighton.'

Tessa laughed.

'You've been busy. Supper sounds great. I'll be down in a minute.'

'You can't have a good long soak in just a minute,' Molly admonished. 'Take an hour.'

Tessa slid under the warm, fragrant water, turned on the whirlpool tap and let out a sigh as the jets massaged her body. Secretly she was glad to have the evening to herself. If Mother went to her latest man friend's, Martin Carson, she wouldn't be home until very late, if at all. Time to herself to catch her breath.

She lifted her left hand out of the soapy water and foam slid away from the large diamond set in tiny black pearls. She wiggled her fingers. It looked just right, just like the man who'd put it there last night, Jerry, whose dark eyes had looked so eloquently into hers as he asked her to be his wife and then kissed her with such exciting, sensual passion when she said yes.

He'd kissed her before but never like last night. Before, there had been a reserve, an aloofness about him, and always their dates had been well out of town, away from the hospital.

'I hate hospital gossip,' he'd said on their first dinner date in a secluded country hotel. 'This is just between you and me. Agreed?'

He'd touched her lips lightly and she'd nodded, told nobody, not even her best friend, Helen, of this entirely unexpected development in her life. At the hospital, she and Jerry were simply polite colleagues with no touch or glance of betrayal. At first she'd thought it odd but after a while it seemed natural and the times they were together took on the heightened excitement of secrecy.

Last night's party was the first time they'd been together at a hospital function and it was obviously deliberate on Jerry's part — his declaration of intent to the world. Later, on their way home, he'd stopped the car, taken her in his arms, kissed her and asked her to marry him. Her breath had caught in her throat, her first emotion surprise, the instinctive reaction almost spoken out loud — why me?

'I love you,' he'd said. 'We'll make a great partnership. Please say yes.'

Before she could speak, his lips claimed hers in a deep, passionate kiss. She was unable to resist. This must be love, she thought, so of course she said yes. That Jerry Talbot should want her was immensely flattering and quite wonderful.

She slid off the ring and dropped it in the soap dish. Mother would be pleased. Jerry had been a protégée of hers from junior doctor to consultant. She respected his brilliance and frequently deferred to his opinion on gynaecological problems.

'Tessa,' Molly called out, 'your mum's on the phone.'

Tessa pulled on a bathrobe and padded to the bedroom phone.

'Hello, Mother. Where are you? Did the seminar go well?'

'Yes, it was useful. Martin met me, and how are you?'

The pause was expectant.

'Uh . . . er . . . I . . . stand by for a shock. I never . . . '

'Come on, Tessa, don't dawdle. I've already guessed. You're engaged, aren't you? And to Jerry Talbot. Congratulations. Wonderful news. Look, I've things to sort out here so do you mind if I stay over at Martin's this evening? But we'll have a celebration dinner tomorrow. It's booked for Enrico's.'

'That'll be nice. Just the two of us?'

'Don't be silly,' Margaret said. 'With Jerry and Martin, of course.'

'But Jerry's in Brighton. The conference.'

'He can leave it for the evening. I fixed it this morning from Milan.'

'But you didn't know this morning. How on earth could you have known? It only happened last night.'

'Jerry discussed it with me last week. You've kept it pretty quiet.'

'You talked it over last week?' Tessa choked.

'Rather sweet really, asking my permission. I thought that sort of thing went out with Queen Victoria, but Jerry is an unusual man. You're a lucky girl. I never expected such good fortune for you. I gladly gave him the go-ahead. Just the sort of son-in-law I always wanted. Well done, Tessa. I didn't think you had it in you quite frankly.'

'Mother, you . . . '

The sound of a doorbell, voices and laughter drifted down the line from Martin Carson's penthouse flat in Hyde Park.

'Must go. Martin's organised a surprise welcome-home party.'

'You've only been away three days, and he didn't invite me.'

Tessa's childish remark was involuntary.

'Darling, you hate parties. Look, see you tomorrow. 'Bye for now.'

Tessa shrugged. Par for the course, but she was disappointed. She'd looked forward to lobbing her own bombshell at her mother. Now it was a damp squib.

She slept soundly that night and had to struggle up through deep layers of sleep to focus on Molly's voice.

'It's him, Mr Talbot. He wants to talk to you.'

Tessa blinked at the alarm clock. Seven o'clock! She wasn't due to work until noon and she'd hoped for a long lie-in.

Molly put a mug of coffee on the table.

'I told him you were asleep but he said he had to talk to you.'

'OK, Molly, I'm awake. Thanks.'

'Breakfast?' Molly asked hopefully.

'Why not? I shan't get back to sleep again now.'

'Right, bacon and egg coming up.'

Tessa picked up the phone.

'Hi,' she said tentatively.

'Darling, I'm sorry to wake you. I couldn't get through to you last night and I've a presentation at eight-thirty. Non-stop after that.'

'What's the problem?'

'Problem? There isn't one unless I mistook your answer the other night. You did say yes, didn't you?'

'Yes, yes, I did. You . . . um . . . said you loved me.'

She was curiously shy about it. It seemed unreal and she was still a little in awe of him.

'Tessa, aren't you awake properly? Of course I did and we're getting married as soon as possible.'

'Married!'

She hadn't thought beyond the fact that Jerry loved her.

'It usually follows. We'll talk tonight. I wish it was just the two of us but your mother . . . '

'Yes. You can get away?'

'Certainly. It's a dull conference but I'll have to be back for the closing session. Must go! See you tonight, and Tessa, remember, I love you.'

'Me, too.'

Carefully she replaced the receiver and leaned back against the pillows. Her heart was beating fast, her stomach churning and not just in anticipation of Molly's bacon and eggs. She reached for her coffee cup and took a calming gulp. The phone rang again. Bad news. Sister Bedford had called in sick and could Tessa cover from as soon as possible? It was going to be a long day with no time for relaxing beauty treatments in preparation for the evening.

Professor Margaret Ferguson, on the other hand, looked as though she'd spent all day in a beauty salon instead of clearing a back-log of appointments. She met Tessa on the doorstep on her return home.

'Heavens, Tessa, you look dreadful. Why are you so late? We're due at Enrico's in half an hour.'

'Staff shortage. I'll have a quick shower and wash my hair.'

Margaret shrugged. She had boundless energy. Without it she'd never have climbed to the top of her profession in general medicine yet she still managed to chair several medical charities and squeeze in a full social life, currently revolving around her latest man, Martin Carson, a wealthy banker.

He'd organised tonight's celebration at one of London's top hotels and his personal chauffeur took Tessa and her mother to the restaurant. Tessa's heart jolted as the man sitting in the bar stood up to greet them. Jerry's dark good looks were enhanced by his immaculate suit and dark silk shirt. He took her hands in his, pulled her towards him and kissed her on the lips.

'You're beautiful,' he murmured. 'You must be proud of her, Margaret.'

'Yes of course.'

Margaret looked bemused, as though the concept of a beautiful daughter didn't tally with her own opinion. Tessa was quite attractive on a good day but never beautiful, and far too thin. In contrast, she herself was strikingly, almost flamboyantly handsome — tall, graceful, erect, her dark hair showing not a trace of grey. Martin Carson observed her with obvious admiration but dutifully kissed Tessa on the cheek before placing his arm around Margaret.

'Congratulations, Tessa and Jerry.'

A waiter placed a magnum of champagne on the table and at a nod from Martin opened it and filled four crystal goblets. He raised his glass.

'To a long and happy life. I'm sure you'll have a wonderful future together, and you're acquiring a great mother-in-law in the package. Lucky man, Jerry.'

'I couldn't be more delighted, and we're dying to hear your plans over supper,' Margaret enthused.

Tessa's head was devoid of plans, and the rich food, wine, and a long working day had a soporific effect. She willed herself alert as Jerry's plans for their future whirled around the table.

'We'll marry as soon as possible. I can't see any point in waiting, can you, Tessa? And as to the wedding itself . . . oh, a huge affair. It'll take time to organise. The guest list will be enormous. Families, colleagues, contacts . . . '

'Contacts?' Tessa broke in swiftly. 'Why should contacts come to my wedding? I don't want a big affair, preferably as little fuss as possible. I hardly know all those Scottish cousins on Dad's side, and I didn't know you had any family, Jerry.'

'Scattered round the globe. There's a lot you don't know about me, Tessa, but we've a lifetime to put that right. My parents are long dead as I told you but I've siblings, aunts, cousins.'

Tessa was surprised. He'd never mentioned any family, indeed Jerry Talbot's reputation was of a loner, an aloof, contained personality, affable and hard-working at the hospital, with his private life very private, typified by the secrecy of his courtship of her. He laughed at her expression.

'Don't be alarmed. Two brothers are in Australia, and both my sisters work in Japan. We don't meet often. I'm sure they'll come to our wedding though, to meet you.'

'I hope so,' Tessa said trying to swallow a yawn. 'Couldn't we go to an exotic island and get married there? I've seen so few places in the world.'

'Out of the question,' Margaret said. 'You'll disappoint so many people, but a honeymoon on some marvellous Caribbean island would be lovely.'

Tessa's eyes closed.

'Hey,' Jerry nudged her, 'you're about

to keel over on to the coffee. I'll take you home.'

'Surely not, the night's young,' Margaret demurred.

Jerry took Tessa's arm.

'It's been a wonderful evening. A great meal, thank you, Martin, but Tessa's tired and I have to be back at the conference pretty well at crack of dawn tomorrow.'

'If you must,' Margaret said with a frown. 'Martin and I thought we might go on somewhere for a while.'

Jerry was already leading Tessa out of the crowded restaurant. The waiter brought her coat and a taxi appeared miraculously as they stepped out into the night air.

'You didn't want to stay, did you?' he asked solicitously.

'No. I had to work double shift today. I'm sorry.'

He turned her to him.

'Don't be. I've been wanting to do this all evening.'

His kiss was sweet and gentle then

deepened into the passion she knew he was capable of. She responded, enjoying the sensation of his lips on hers, his hands caressing her, melting her to him.

'I love you, Tess, and we'll be married soon. We will honeymoon on a tropical island. I know just the place, a beautiful hotel on a paradise island, sunshine, fantastic food and wine, snorkelling, diving and best of all, just the two of us.'

He kissed her again and as she closed her eyes she visualised that island, a warm paradise of love to share with Jerry.

2

Thousands of miles away, in a different time zone, torrential rain lashed across the island of St Christos, a tiny pin-prick of land standing between the Atlantic Ocean and the Caribbean. The island hardly warranted a mapmaker's attention, it was just one of many islands strung away from South America.

Few knew or cared about St Christos which was not on the glittering tourist cruise circuit. The large ships avoided the island's protective reefs which could churn up mighty breakers on its Atlantic side, while the sheer cliffs of the Caribbean side made landing even a small boat unpredictable and hazardous to those unfamiliar with St Christos's hidden coves and landing stages.

If a visitor had braved the reefs on this rain-swept afternoon he or she would have presumed the island's inhabitants had fled. The streets and dirt tracks were deserted, the spice fields and banana plantations empty. The day was a day of mourning, a day set aside to say farewell to the man who had been St Christos's leader, to some of the older men and women their physical and spiritual inspiration for over half a century.

Six men bore the coffin away from the simple white wood church, the mourners filing into a black snaking ribbon behind the pall bearers. The procession followed a rough track through a coconut grove alongside a beach before climbing up to the cliff top where Gordon Ferguson would be laid to rest in the burial ground which had been exclusively prepared for him. A stone cross would mark his grave and smaller stones ringed the plot which would be a future place of pilgrimage for the islanders.

The minister and island dignitaries headed the mourners just as Gordon had planned every other detail of his funeral, from the simple service to the celebratory wake to be held in the town that evening. The man entrusted to carry out these final directions walked behind the minister's group.

He and the girl accompanying him were the only Europeans in the procession, the rest native to the island together with outsiders from neighbouring islands. The man was tall, his wet shirt clinging to his body showing broad, muscular shoulders, his hair slicked darkly to his head. The big umbrella he carried shielded the girl from the downpour.

Alex Ross held his umbrella higher.

'Fitting weather,' he bent to whisper to the girl. 'Gordon probably engineered this — weeping skies for his passing.'

She looked up sharply.

'That's a bit fanciful. How much farther is it?'

'About a mile to the burial ground.'

'A mile! I'm already soaked through.'

'You'll have to stick it out. You can't turn back now. They'd see it as a mark of disrespect.'

Suddenly the grey veil lifted magically as swiftly as it had descended, and a watery sun grew stronger as the wind changed direction to scatter the storm clouds.

'See, sunshine as well, couldn't be more appropriate.'

Alex Ross lowered the umbrella as the crowd behind him began to sing, softly and reverently at first, gradually becoming louder, more cheerful, so by the time the crowd had reached Gordon Ferguson's final resting place the atmosphere was almost carnival.

'Great,' Alex said and looked up to the sky. 'Just what he ordered, rain for sorrow at his passing, the sun for the future of St Christos. Mission accomplished.'

'You're mad,' the girl said. 'I'll be glad when this is all over.'

'I think,' Alex said solemnly as the coffin was finally lowered into the

23

waiting grave on the hillside looking out to sea, 'that this is just the beginning of another story, and with the old man gone, who knows where it will end? We can only hope he made the right decision for the future.'

His tone implied the opposite. Jane Horton shivered.

'I think the whole thing's weird, primitive. I'll be glad when we leave.'

Alex Ross declined to comment. He had too many other things on his mind, not least the legacy Gordon had left him.

★   ★   ★

Tessa stretched out her legs to the sun, kicked off her shoes and lifted her face to the spring sunshine, revelling in its warmth and the joy of just being outdoors in the park, away for an hour from the hospital.

'Hi, there. You managed to escape!'

'Helen. Thank goodness. I was beginning to think you wouldn't make it.'

'I was determined this time. I just had to see you and the telephone's no substitute for a real talk.'

Helen Lonsdale surveyed her friend critically.

'Not exactly starry-eyed but you look good. Now, tell me all about it.'

'After a long morning stint in the ward I do feel bleary-eyed rather than starry.'

'I couldn't believe it. When I got back from Newcastle, your message on the answerphone, engaged, and to Jerry Talbot. How, when, why? And why didn't I at least know you were going out with him? And are you really getting married in August? Why didn't you tell me?'

'I'm truly sorry but you were away and then I was so busy, but I left messages. I phoned your mother.'

'Yes, yes,' Helen said, waving her hand impatiently, 'I know all that. I want to know the details — you, him, when, how? Come on, I've got to be back on the ward soon.'

Tessa smiled. Helen was her best friend, a friendship which had started in childhood, and on to schooldays before their paths diverged, Helen to fulfil her long-time ambition to be a doctor, Tessa, much to her mother's annoyance, a career in nursing. It was possibly the only time in her life she'd stood out against her mother — and won!

It had been a tough fight. Margaret Ferguson moved heaven and earth to persuade her daughter to go to medical school and Tessa had just as stubbornly refused and had never regretted it. She had never envied Helen's frantic work life.

'Well?' Helen looked at her watch. 'I've fifteen minutes to hear the bare bones then we'll make a date to meet up for dinner very soon.'

'OK. Jerry and I had been seeing each other for a while . . . well, a few weeks. He doesn't like hospital gossip so we kept it quiet, that's all, and I see so little of you these days. I would have told you.'

'Sure, and you're . . . um . . . happy?'

'Of course I'm happy. Who wouldn't be? It's so exciting. I can't really believe it. You'll like him.'

'He's an attractive man. I met him at a pharmacy convention. He's got a fantastic reputation, a workaholic, very dedicated.'

'I know.'

'I bet your mother's delighted.'

'She is, finally.'

'She's never approved of your other blokes.'

Tessa laughed.

'Others? You mean the love of my younger life, poor old Geoff Hoskins? She demolished him very quickly. I've never quite forgiven her for that.'

For a moment the girls were quiet then Helen pulled a pack of sandwiches and a can of juice from her bag.

'OK, here's a celebration picnic, best I could do in the time. We'll make up for it as soon as possible, and when am I going to meet again this paragon of a husband-to-be?'

'Soon. Why didn't I think of a picnic?

You always did have the bright ideas. Mother said I used to tag along after you like Tinkerbell's shadow.'

'What a horrid thing to say, with due respect to your respected ma. Of course you didn't tag along. Why do you always do yourself down, Tess? Jerry Talbot's a lucky guy and I'll tell him so when I see him.'

Impulsively she hugged her friend.

'It'll be great, I know it will.'

She spurted open the can and fought with the plastic sandwich box.

'Here's to you both,' she said and passed the can and a limp sandwich. 'A great future, and I'll kill you if I'm not to be a bridesmaid.'

'Oh, Helen, who else? Thanks.'

'So, how long before the day?'

'Just over eight weeks. Mother's already in fifth gear.'

'I bet. Wow!'

The friends eyed each other with something akin to alarm.

⋆   ⋆   ⋆

The feeling buzzing Alex Ross as he spun his motor boat towards St Christos was frustration, something he hadn't felt since leaving his high-powered job in London's financial market years ago. He loved the laid-back, slow pace of the island but there were times when he wanted to shake the place into action, and this was one of them. It was a month since Gordon Ferguson had been laid to rest on his favourite hilltop and still the island's future remained uncertain. Gordon's words rang in his head.

'See to it fast, my boy. Get the lawyers moving. I've picked a top London firm. Curtis is too close to the island so it's up to you.'

Alex tied up his boat at the small landing jetty. A knot of islanders greeted him with enthusiasm.

'Hey there, Alex man, how ya doing? Any news?'

'Not a thing. That's why I'm here, to see Curtis.'

A tall, powerfully-built man raised his

29

hand in greeting.

'And here I am to meet you, to escort you personally. Bella's got lunch at Gordon's old house but first we'll do the business down in my office.'

The two men shook hands, climbed into a battered Jeep, and Curtis Ollivière, St Christos's only lawyer and part-time taxi service when business was slow, drove off with a wave to the bystanders.

The road from town was a dirt track lined on each side with a blazing profusion of orange and scarlet blooms. As they drove past a long, low, ranch-style building Curtis gave three horn blasts. He grinned at Alex.

'Just to let Bella know you've arrived.'

'Everything OK at the house?' Alex asked.

Curtis shrugged.

'Bella's bored and she misses looking after Gordon. Everything's slowed down since he went, practically a full stop.'

Alex laughed.

'St Christos wasn't exactly a candidate for the rat-race when Gordon was alive but I do notice no-one seems to be working in the fields.'

'People aren't sure of the future any more. They don't see any point exerting themselves for nothing.'

'How d'you know it's for nothing? Gordon wanted things to go on exactly as before. No reason why not.'

'No leader any more, no direction. Rumours grow. The main story's that the island's up for tourist development. Big American company got its eye on us.'

'You know that's nonsense. Just what Gordon would loathe.'

'Then why didn't he write a more watertight and sensible will?'

Curtis brought the vehicle to a juddering, dusty halt outside one of the town's few stone-built buildings.

'But he did. The conditions of the legacy are fairly specific,' Alex protested as he jumped down.

'Mmm. I'm afraid a really smart lawyer could find plenty of loopholes. I did warn him.'

In Curtis's ramshackle office an overhead fan whined and whirred. The lawyer produced cool beer from an ice-box, snapped the tops off, handed one to Alex and drank his down in one gulp.

'OK, progress on Gordon's last will and testament. As joint executors you and I are duty bound to carry out his wishes for the disposal of St Christos and then make sure the new owner carries on along the same lines as Gordon.'

'Agreed, morally bound, too. Death-bed promise, remember.'

'I surely do. I'll never make one again. I didn't think it would be so difficult. Gordon's mistake was to use a London law firm. I can't get anywhere with them. They were fine to begin with then suddenly they turned elusive, didn't return my calls, long delays in answering letters, some story about verifying the legatee and checking the legality of the conditions. They're stalling, Alex, and I'd like to know why. The future of our island's at stake here. The fool I talked to last in London doesn't even know where St Christos is, or so he made out.'

He pushed a file over to Alex.

'There's the record of progress to date and it won't take you long to read it. Then you'll see there's only one thing to do if we're to settle this as Gordon Ferguson wished.'

Alex took the file, glanced at it and frowned.

'That's all?'

'That's it. I'd say nil progress. Nothing else for it. You'll have to go yourself. Go to London, rattle the lawyers, contact the family yourself. I can't think why we haven't done that before now.'

'You know why. Gordon was so cautious. The lawyers are supposed to check out the family, see if they're still alive and morally upright. It was fifteen years ago when he made that will and there's been no contact since.'

Alex tipped his chair forward and took another beer.

'I left London to get away from the rat-race and I don't want to go back there. It's not necessary, just keep on faxing what's their name? McGuire and Kendall's? Keep on until you get some action.'

'You can see from the file I've done just that. It's your turn now. Surely you want to see your folks, and Jane? Funny sort of love affair, thousands of miles apart.'

'My folks are in Scotland, the other end of the UK from London. They were over a couple of months ago, remember, and as for Jane, I've a feeling she won't be back here. She has her work in London, mine's on St Marques with a business partner who won't be overjoyed if I go off again.'

'He won't mind. He's your cousin, family, he'll understand. Go on, Alex. Things have just stalled here and I can't kick-start them. Those London lawyers've got me down as a no-account, hick, back-country lawyer.'

Alex sighed.

'OK, I'll think about it. Now, let's get to Bella's. Cheer her up.'

'Just the sight of you'll bring back that lovely smile of hers.'

'I can't stay long. We're stacked out with bookings. Seems like the world wants to scuba dive in the Caribbean.'

'Good for business, and best of luck in London.'

'Who says I'm going?'

'You will because you promised the old man to steer this through.'

As it turned out it wasn't only his promise to Gordon Ferguson that propelled Alex across the Atlantic next day. Back at the diving school on St Marques he ran with his cousin, Tony, there were two messages, one from Jane needing to talk, and more worrying, a call from his mother. His father had had a sudden heart attack. He should come home at once.

'Of course you must go,' Tony reassured him. 'I've already booked you on the overnight flight from Barbados and there's a charter on standby at the airstrip here.'

'I feel bad leaving you again when we're so busy.'

'Forget it. Providentially a young guy's turned up looking for casual work, a student who's also a first-class diving instructor. So get packing and give my love to everybody in Edinburgh.'

'I will. Thanks.'

He gave a deep sigh.

'I just hate to leave here when everything's going so well.'

'You have to go and we'll still be here when you get back. I'm sure Uncle Bill will pull through. He's as tough as old boots.'

'I hope you're right, and I'll tie up the St Christos business as fast as possible. It's been left too long already.'

3

Douglas McGuire, junior partner in the London law firm of McGuire and Kendall, leaned back in his chair. Alex Ross leaned forward trying to suppress his irritation. The dark-suited lawyer typified everything Alex had left the City for and he'd kept Alex waiting for half an hour and now had spent ten minutes fielding his questions with an air of bland superiority.

Jet-lagged, weary and anxious about his father, Alex tried to keep calm.

'Look, Mr McGuire, I've had a long, tiring flight and I don't want to hear that the matter's in hand because patently it isn't and I don't understand why. It's a simple enough matter, to implement Gordon Ferguson's will, give us the go-ahead so we, myself and Curtis Ollivière on St Christos, can get things moving on the island.'

'Not so simple. Don't forget, Mr Ferguson's instruction was quite clear, vet the family, not just the heir.'

'Then why in goodness' name haven't you done it?'

'We've made progress but this is a strange clause, not at all usual.'

'So if it's out of your field we'll take it elsewhere.'

Alex reached across the desk for the papers the lawyer was holding.

'No.'

The file was snapped shut and slipped swiftly into a drawer. Imperceptibly, the key to the drawer was turned and the Ferguson file was under lock and key! Alex was puzzled. There was something not quite right, a tension out of proportion to the proving of a simple will. He looked more closely at Doug McGuire but the man was smiling now. It didn't fool Alex.

'Look, Mr Ross, I'll be frank with you. My father founded this firm, worked hard all his life. Now he's retired.'

Alex was even more puzzled as he tried to tie up McGuire senior's retirement and Gordon's will.

'My father is quite old, should have retired years ago but he insisted on staying on until . . . well, to be blunt, we had to insist. He was making mistakes, costing us. In short we had to seek medical opinion to convince him he was no longer up to running a busy law practice such as this.'

Alex was bewildered as McGuire continued.

'One of the cases that . . . ah . . . fell by the wayside was . . . '

'Gordon Ferguson's will. Ah, I see.'

'Exactly, but now it's in hand. We've made progress and should be ready to move on in ten days.'

'Ten days! That won't do. I've to be back on the island within the week.'

Alex crossed his fingers and prayed his dad would be well enough for him to leave with a clear conscience, well within a week.

'Out of the question. I can't hang

about that long but at least I can make contact with the family, see for myself.'

'That wouldn't be wise.' Doug McGuire's face was set. 'In the circumstances, I think we can move things along. Say a week?'

'Three days,' Alex said and prepared to leave. 'I have to drive up to Scotland and hope to be back on Thursday. That's the day I want to meet Gordon's heir, otherwise I shall have to look for another lawyer.'

'That won't be necessary, Mr Ross. Leave a contact number with my secretary and she will keep you informed.'

A phone call reassured Alex his father was stable though still in intensive care. His mother's soft voice was calm.

'Things are fine. Don't come rushing up here. Get a night's rest. Why don't you fly? It's a long drive. Ginny will meet you at the airport.'

'I've already hired a car. I'll see. Don't worry.'

'Don't you. We're all looking forward to seeing you.'

He was relieved. It was stupid to think of driving, he realised. He'd been so distracted he'd automatically picked up a car at Heathrow, intending to drive straight from there, but on a whim had called in at McGuire and Kendall's on the off-chance of seeing someone, and he was glad now he'd started the ball rolling. He phoned Jane on his mobile.

'Alex! You're in London? There was no need to come . . . '

'I had to. Dad's ill.'

'I'm sorry. Serious?'

'Yes, but he'll be OK. Can we meet later? I'm going to Edinburgh tomorrow.'

'No. If I see you I might change my mind and I've decided I'm not coming back to St Marques. Not my kind of life. I belong here in the City.'

'Meet me. We can talk at least.'

He spoke without much conviction. He'd been expecting it. Jane was a city girl. The island made her nervous. She'd never have settled.

'No, Alex, don't spoil it. No regrets.

It was fine, but now it is over. My love to your parents. 'Bye.'

And that was it, the end of a less-than-perfect relationship — on, off, on, off, so many times as their life styles drifted poles apart. Sad. There was a little hurt from the rejection but relief, too.

He was still tired and anxious about home but his heart was lighter as he drove his hired car towards Highgate. To see the house would be something and if his luck was in, someone might be home. He had absolutely no intention of sticking to absurd McGuire rules and he was very keen to meet the Ferguson family. He was startled by the opulence of the Ferguson house. No shortage of money there!

Molly answered the ring.

'The Ferguson house?' Alex inquired.

'Aye. Which one would you be wanting?'

'Er . . . any one of the family.'

'There are only two of them. Jim, Mr Ferguson, died years ago. There's Mrs

Margaret Ferguson, professor. She's out of town right now, then there's Tessa, the daughter.'

'Where will Tessa be?'

'At work. Who are you? What do you want with them?'

Molly approved of the man, tall, good-looking in an outdoor way, though you never knew these days. She'd held on to the door ready to slam in the nice young man's face if her judgement was awry.

'I'm sorry.'

Alex produced a card.

Molly read it aloud.

'Alex Ross, St Marques Watersports, Scuba, Fishing, Diving.'

She handed it back.

'Not much call for that here.'

'Of course not, it's just to . . . well, never mind. I'm a . . . a family friend,' he hesitated. 'A friend of Gordon Ferguson.'

'Doesn't mean anything to me. Lots of folk called Ferguson. What's your connection?'

'Quite distant. Is it possible to see the

young one, Tessa?'

'She works at City Hospital. She's terribly busy, I don't think . . . '

'Sure, you're right. I'll call back again. Nice to meet you.'

'You, too. Shall I say you called?'

'No, nothing. I'll be in touch. Thanks for your help.'

Molly held the door wide as he ran down the steps to his car.

★ ★ ★

Tessa had picked up a patient file for Jerry from nearby St Judes Hospital and was returning to City Hospital. As usual she was pushed for time but for once the back streets were comparatively quiet.

She glanced at her watch, not bad, ten minutes. That moment of inattention caused her to overshoot the left-hand turn towards the hospital carpark. Swinging wide to correct, she skidded over the centre lane and crashed into an oncoming car! The sound of scrunching metal and tinkling glass told her there must be some damage but, securely held by her seatbelt, she herself was unhurt.

'Blast!'

She'd be even later and by ill fortune it was a male driver in the other car. Obviously he'd be furious. It was her fault and she braced herself. The man got out and came towards her.

'I'm sorry,' she placated. 'I missed the turning. It was stupid. I should have carried on and turned round.'

He noticed the eyes first, deep, deep blue, almost cobalt, expressive, distressed now, anxious. He smiled.

'We all make mistakes. London's traffic is horrendous. I'd forgotten. Look, we're causing a jam. I think our cars are drivable. Mine's a hired car. We need to change addresses, insurers. I'll turn round and follow you.'

Tessa blinked. Not a cross word, no anger!

'Thanks. The hospital carpark's over there. We should find a corner.'

He followed Tessa to the hospital.

'Not a great deal of damage though I think you may need a new off-side wing. I'll give you my folks' address in Scotland. I'm just visiting.'

'I'm sorry,' Tessa said again, scribbling her information on a notepad. 'I was in such a rush. I'm late but thanks so much.'

'What for?'

'For being so nice about my driving into you.'

'It was an accident, not something you did on purpose.'

He took the folded paper and put it in his pocket.

'Do you work here?'

'Yes, and I'm getting later by the minute. Thanks.'

She glanced at his card.

'Alex Ross, thanks again. 'Bye.'

And she was off, running across the carpark.

'Wait, do you know . . . ?' he called but she was out of earshot.

Alex shrugged and decided to abandon the search. He'd meet up with the

Fergusons soon enough. He hated to admit it but probably McGuire was right — best to meet the family with a lawyer present. He decided to find a hotel, ring home, snatch an hour or two of sleep, then drive up to Edinburgh early next morning.

The insistent shrilling of the hotel phone startled him out of a deep sleep.

'Alex, it's Mother.'

This time the voice was shaky.

'Your father's worsened since you last phoned. They think you should come right away. I'm so sorry.'

'I'm on my way. Good job I did get a car. I can start off right now. See you soon.'

The car hire firm promised to deliver a replacement car to the hotel within the hour. Alex hurriedly scribbled details of the accident and pushed it in an envelope with Tessa's note. He looked closer at the note.

'Good heavens! She was Tessa Ferguson herself.'

The address was the one he'd called

at that morning. So he'd met her after all and by the strangest of coincidences. However, his family was his first priority. Tessa Ferguson would keep.

Snapping shut his bag he went downstairs to check out, collect the new car and head North, praying he wouldn't be too late.

★   ★   ★

Tessa shuffled through the piles of papers with growing dismay. Guest lists yards long, caterers' estimates, florists' brochures, photographers . . .

'Mother, you've gone to a great deal of trouble and how you found the time I . . . but I . . . we don't really want such a huge affair. I don't know half the people you're inviting. Can't we scale it down?'

'Very doubtful, and I don't want to. Don't I have a say? You're my only daughter and it's my only chance to plan the perfect wedding. And there are many useful contacts on the guest lists, invaluable to Jerry in his career.'

'But it's my wedding. I want to marry Jerry, not further his career. Jerry?'

She turned to her fiancé who tactfully poured the three of them a glass of wine each.

'No need to quarrel,' he murmured. 'I can see why Margaret wants to make this an occasion and as she says it's her one chance. Isn't the important thing about the day the fact that we end up as man and wife?'

He leaned over and kissed her — and Tessa's heart melted.

'I don't care if there are four guests or four hundred. It's you I want, but if it gives Margaret pleasure to organise the day,' he shrugged, 'what's the harm? And I want as many people as possible to see my beautiful bride.'

Tessa knew when she was beaten.

'All right, go ahead, but that's the limit. Two hundred guests.'

'And a few others at the evening reception.'

As Margaret pulled out another piece

of paper, Tessa put her head in her hands and groaned. Just then, Molly came in.

'Telephone for either Miss Tessa or Mrs Professor in the downstairs study.'

'Either of us?' Margaret frowned. 'That must be a mistake. I'm expecting a call. Thank you, Molly. Don't go away,' she warned Tessa and Jerry.

'I don't think I can stand it,' Tessa said and took Jerry's hand. 'Can't we just elope, go to Gretna Green, or better still, to the honeymoon island you were telling me about? Let's fly off and marry there. If Mother wants to come she can, and Martin, just as long as they leave right after the ceremony.'

'Darling,' Jerry replied as he took her in his arms, 'we can't do that. You'll love the day when it comes, all eyes on you, the centre of attention.'

'That's not for me. That's Mother's style, not mine.'

'You undersell yourself.'

He kissed her, and then went on, 'I don't know why. You're beautiful, talented, and can hold your own with anyone. What's the problem?'

He was genuinely puzzled. He admired Margaret Ferguson tremendously but she was the last kind of woman he'd ever want to live with, her ego was too large to allow room for another. He wondered about Tessa's father and what sort of marriage that had been.

'You live in your mother's shadow, Tess, and it's time you got out from under. Be your own person.'

'You're right but it's never bothered me. She is just so brilliant.'

He drew her closer and she could feel his heart beating against her.

'We'll be a good partnership, Tessa. With you to help me I can build up a wonderful private practice. With my expertise and your nursing skills we can . . . '

Tessa moved away.

'My nursing skills? But I'm a paediatric nurse. You'd need a specialist.'

'Not really. Your skills are transferable and you're getting experience on obstetrics and gynaecology right now. I thought you were enjoying it.'

'I am, but you've always known I want to work in paediatrics.'

'You mean to continue with that after we're married?'

'Of course. Why not?'

Absently, Jerry picked up one of Margaret's scattered papers.

'Is that really what the church flowers will cost?'

'Jerry,' Tess snapped and snatched the paper from him, 'this is important. I need to carry on with my own career for a while. Maybe when we have a family, but even then . . . '

Panic shortened her breath as she realised she'd never thought much beyond the fact that Jerry loved her and wanted to marry her. They'd never discussed the future, mapped out a strategy. Did other couples, or did most people arrive at this stage, wedding preparations well in hand, only to

realise an important issue was unre-
solved? And she could see that to Jerry
it was an important issue.

'Jerry,' she pleaded, 'it's not that
important. You have good nurses, you
don't need me. I've always wanted to
work.'

'There's no need to argue. If that's
how you feel there's no more to be said.
I assumed we would work together. I
was mistaken.'

Pointedly he looked at his watch.

'I must go. I've a meeting and I don't
want to be late.'

Tessa put her hand on his arm just as
Margaret came back into the room. She
looked puzzled, and barely noticed the
tension between them.

'A most extraordinary phone call,
from a lawyer called McGuire. He
asked all sorts of questions, wanted to
speak to you, Tess. I told him you were
immersed in wedding plans. He also
asked about your father. I couldn't
believe it. Jim's been dead nearly ten
years.'

'What was it about? Sit down,' Jerry said. 'You look quite shocked.'

'Thank you. Not shocked, some sixth sense, a premonition.'

'It can't be anything dreadful or he would have told you,' Tessa said.

'He wants us to go to his office tomorrow, or could he come and see us here tomorrow evening?'

'I can't possibly get time off tomorrow,' Tessa said.

'Nor me, I have a full list,' Margaret added.

'I think you should settle for evening then I can be here with you,' Jerry said firmly.

'He did say strictly family.'

'And what am I, bar a few weeks?'

'I'd be grateful,' Margaret said, 'and maybe I'll ask Martin. He's more used to dealing with lawyers than I am.'

Tessa was astounded to see her brisk, no-nonsense mother curiously undermined, almost vulnerable, something she'd never associated with

Margaret Ferguson. It occurred to her that perhaps the McGuire person had told her mother something she was keeping to herself, for the moment.

4

The two men had arranged to meet outside the Fergusons' home. Alex was due to fly back to Barbados the next evening. His father had made a good recovery, and was pronounced by his doctor to be out of danger.

Alex was still reeling from the shock of seeing his father, who had never suffered a day's illness, white and immobile in hospital. He seemed to have shrunk from the big bluff dad he'd known for ever. He'd wanted to stay on but everyone urged him to go back to the Caribbean and stop worrying.

In the end Alex had agreed and phoned Douglas McGuire who, to Alex's surprise, was forthcoming and positive.

'Everything's fine, Mr Ross. I'm as eager as you to finalise this. Tomorrow evening I'll meet you outside the

Ferguson home. I've spoken to Professor Ferguson and look forward to meeting her and her daughter, Tessa.'

Alex decided not to tell him he'd already met Tessa quite by chance. There was nothing to be gained from that.

As he sat in his hired car in the gracious, tree-lined street in Highgate, Alex's mind was already back on the island of St Marques. Once the St Christos business was settled he could give all his attention to the blossoming diving venture. A knock on the window brought him back to London and Douglas McGuire. The two men shook hands. McGuire smiled.

'All well in Scotland?' he enquired politely.

'Fine, thanks. I'm flying back to Barbados tomorrow evening.'

'Right, let's go then. I think the Fergusons are in for a shock. Whether or not it will be an altogether pleasant one remains to be seen.'

'I hope for the sake of the islanders

it'll be a pleasant one. Much depends on the Ferguson reaction,' Alex said grimly.

Molly met them with unconcealed curiosity, especially when she recognised Alex.

'In the library, all four of them. Shall I bring you coffee or something stronger?'

'Coffee would be fine,' both men agreed.

'All four?' McGuire queried.

'Yes, you'll see.'

She showed them into the library and withdrew reluctantly. Margaret Ferguson stood up. Douglas went to meet her.

'Professor Ferguson, I presume. I'm Douglas McGuire and this is Alex Ross, chief executor of Gordon Ferguson's will.'

Alex's eyes went straight to Tessa.

'Goodness, we've already met,' she said. 'The car accident by the hospital and you were so unfazed by it all. I hope it's all sorted.'

'There wasn't a problem. It was a hire car and they replaced it.'

'What a coincidence. You'd never believe we'd meet again so soon.'

'Well, yes, I did. I was actually looking for you and I . . . '

'That was unwise, Mr Ross. I did warn you,' McGuire interrupted with a glare at Alex.

'No harm done. I'd no idea I'd bumped into Tessa Ferguson. Our cars collided, a minor accident. We exchanged insurance details and it was only later I discovered Tessa was Tessa Ferguson.'

'Would someone please explain what is going on?' Margaret said crossly. 'What has Mr . . . er . . . Ross's chance meeting with Tessa to do with why you're both here?'

Martin Carson said coolly, 'Shouldn't we be getting down to the purpose of this visit? We're all busy people.'

'And you are?' McGuire asked.

'A family friend, here to protect the interests of Professor Ferguson and her daughter.'

59

'I can protect our own interests thank you, and we don't know yet there's anything to protect,' Tessa said as she drew Jerry forward. 'This is Jerry Talbot, my fiancé. I asked him to be here.'

McGuire looked doubtful, but Alex said, 'I can't see a problem.'

'Right, we'll get on then. May I?'

He sat at a small table and opened his briefcase. Alex sat where he could watch Tessa, and appraise the fiancé, a guy who looked every inch a successful professional, good-looking, too, definitely with charisma he thought ruefully.

The small audience settled and became still as statues as they listened to the lawyer's preamble to the will.

'Gordon Ferguson came to see my father some years ago. He owned some property which he wished to pass into safe hands after his death. This property was so important to him he wanted to be sure it would go to the right person, someone who thought as he did as to the future of that property. But Mr

Ferguson had had no contact with his immediate family for years and was uneasy about bequeathing his lands to someone who knew nothing about . . . '

'Lands?' Martin interrupted. 'Is this an estate then?'

'All in good time,' McGuire reproved. 'As I said there was no family he knew intimately, that is until some twenty years ago when his nephew, Jim Ferguson, took a trip, to see his long-lost uncle.'

'Jim what?'

Margaret was dumbfounded. Her husband had never mentioned the trip. Surely she would have known.

The lawyer pressed on.

'That was his first visit to the Caribbean, followed by a second, longer one, three years later. On that second visit, he stayed two months, getting to know his uncle and his property.'

'Mother, that was when you went to the States for almost a year. I remember Dad talked to me about going on a trip. He told me about it, wanted to take me.

I was at boarding school. You wouldn't let me leave school and I hated you for that.'

'Tessa!' Margaret said, shocked.

'I'm sorry, Mother, but I was only eleven. I wasn't happy at that school and that trip represented an escape to paradise. I remember now. I hated Dad, too, because he didn't take me with him. I had to shut it all out,' she said flatly, 'because I couldn't bear it. Eventually the memory of that island faded and vanished. I'm sorry. You touched a nerve, Mr McGuire, and I jumped. A reflex action. Please go on.'

During an uneasy coffee break, Martin Carson wandered over to the bookshelves and appeared to have chosen a World Atlas for later reading. Nobody said a word but when Douglas McGuire put down his cup everyone looked up expectantly as he resumed his preamble.

'So you see, Gordon Ferguson eventually did establish a family connection again after being more or less disowned by his immediate Scottish family, for reasons not relevant to this evening's matter. Uncle and nephew apparently grew close, so close that the uncle decided that his nephew was the one person he could trust to run his island after his death.'

'Jim! Run an island?' Margaret exploded. 'Impossible, he couldn't . . . he wouldn't know . . . '

She tailed off and bit her lip, as the lawyer took another document from the folder.

'So now to the actual will which was drawn up soon after Jim Ferguson left the island after his second visit. He made it on one of his rare visits to London. Gordon had seen his nephew, Jim, and told him of his intentions before returning to his island, never to come back to this country. Unfortunately, as McGuire and Kendall learned only recently, Jim Ferguson died soon after that visit. Gordon never knew this and as he became increasingly old and frail it didn't worry him because he had an extra insurance, as you will see.'

He tapped the document on the table in front of him.

'The last will and testament of Gordon Ferguson, of St Christos.'

Martin Carson started. He fingered the atlas on his knee and stared at the lawyer. All attention was on Douglas McGuire who paused to enjoy his dramatic moment, cleared his throat and began to read. It was brief and to the point, bequests and a reminder of duties still to be performed to several of the islanders, an annuity for his loyal and devoted housekeeper, Bella, and finally, 'To my nephew, Jim Ferguson, I bequeath my beloved island of St Christos, for him to own outright and administer as I have indicated to him during his visits here. I trust my nephew will carry out my wishes to the letter. Should he not discharge his obligations as laid down, my executors, Alex Ross and Curtis Ollivière shall revoke this will and management of St

Christos will be their joint responsibility.'

Martin Carson said eagerly, 'So, Jim
Ferguson being dead, the island will
automatically belong to his next of kin,
his wife.'

He looked at Margaret.

'Please, Mr Carson,' the lawyer
rebuked, 'do not jump to conclusions
and allow me to finish. I assume you
know nothing about the law.'

Martin was unabashed. His hands
itched to open the atlas and pin-point
exactly this heaven-sent gift. The
lawyer, however, unused to such brash
interruptions, frowned then carried on
reading to the will's final conclusion.

'In the event of Jim Ferguson pre-
deceasing me, I bequeath St Christos to
my great-niece, Tessa Ferguson, who,
although only a child at the time of my
nephew's visit, I am assured by him has
the latent capabilities to carry out my
wishes regarding the island with integrity and dedication.'

He put the document down after

he'd read the date of its origin.

'You will note the original will is dated ninety-eighty-nine. A precise copy was made ten years later appointing new executors, that is those whom I have named today.'

Under pretext of tidying his papers, he looked at them all. Margaret Ferguson looked stunned, he guessed a rare event. Her companion radiated excitement, the atlas now open, his finger on the page.

'I've got it. It's on the main cruise route. Must be worth a fortune to developers. You're a very lucky woman, Tessa. An heiress!'

'Gordon Ferguson states expressly there must be no mainstream development. That's what he dreaded. There are stringent conditions attached to the inheritance,' Alex Ross said sharply.

Martin exchanged glances with the lawyer and for the first time a look of total understanding passed between them. There were more loopholes in the conditions of Gordon Ferguson's will than in a fishing net. Douglas McGuire knew it by practice. It had been one of his father's last cases and it was a mess and Martin Carson knew it by instinct. They both looked at Tessa. She would be the key factor, she and the attractive-looking guy who had a protective arm around her. How much influence would he have?

Alex Ross looked glum. He didn't like the atmosphere. He sensed tension and problems he didn't begin to understand but he knew now that far from this being the end of his involvement with St Christos, it was merely the beginning. He looked towards Tessa but in her expressive eyes as she exchanged glances with her fiancé there was no clue as to what she was thinking about her unexpected inheritance.

5

The lawyer removed his spectacles, sat back, and waited for his news to take effect.

'Unbelievable,' Martin said first. 'Did the old boy . . . er . . . Gordon, Mr Ferguson, have any idea of the value of his island? It's on line for the best hot spots in the Caribbean, smack on the tourist route. Only last week I was talking to a guy who's desperate to snap up a place like . . . what's it called, St Christos? Wants to develop exclusive hideaways for the very rich. St Christos seems the perfect plum, ripe for picking. You'll have the pick of the most exclusive wedding gear, Tessa, plus all the rest.'

'St Christos is not a plum for picking!' Alex registered his disgust angrily. 'That'd be the last thing Gordon wanted and that's crystal clear in his will. Haven't you listened to a word that's been said? His great niece is the new owner so it'll be up to her.'

Alex tried to keep his voice reasonable but he sensed Martin Carson was bad news and wondered just what influence he had with the Fergusons.

'It will be a family decision, of course.'

Martin turned to Margaret, confirming Alex's fears.

'You would advise Tessa to sell, surely?'

'I don't know. This is a great surprise to me. My husband . . . all those years . . . not a word, not even a hint. Why?'

Tessa opened her mouth to state the obvious — her mother, in pursuit of a glittering career, had become an absentee wife. She recalled that most of her parents' conversations had been about Margaret's train and flight schedules and how Jim could juggle his own modest career as a professional gardening consultant to cover her absence.

'What possible use would Tessa have

69

for a Caribbean island?' Martin urged.

'Perhaps Miss Ferguson has her own views on the matter,' Douglas McGuire interjected mildly.

Tessa started, then took the atlas from Martin and placed it on the table in front of Alex.

'Where exactly?' she asked.

'Here,' he replied and pointed to a speck on the page, 'and here's the inset blow-up.'

A scattered group of islands showed St Christos as the smallest.

'How big?'

'Twelve miles by six, maybe more in overall area. There are a lot of spits and peninsulas. It has a rocky coastline.'

'Tourism potential?'

'Hardly.' Alex laughed. 'A small guest house, three or four rooms if the owner can be bothered to open up. Sometimes Janie will take our surplus divers but it's primitive by western standards.'

'So how does the population exist?'

'Self-sufficiency, and enough export of spices, coconuts and bananas to buy necessities. They get by.' He paused. 'They're happy,' he said a shade defiantly. 'I've compiled as much information on St Christos as there is.'

He passed over a folder.

'My cousin and I operate from St Marques, your nearest neighbour.'

'My island neighbour.' Tessa smiled and handed the atlas to Jerry. 'That sounds good.'

Jerry scanned the map.

'Maybe, but hardly practical as far as your career is concerned. It needs careful thought. Margaret, what do you think? It's more a romantic notion, isn't it?'

'Why, yes.'

She was recovering very slowly from the shock.

'Impractical, of course, like Jim apparently. I can't imagine — was he going to go native on me? I thought I knew the man,' she said quite violently. 'Anyway, it's nothing to do with me although I think Tessa should get rid of it at once. Martin, you reckon it would fetch a good price?'

'Well, it's a little premature to say.'

Tessa spoke quietly to the lawyer.

'Can I sell it? It is mine, mine alone?'

'Yes, it's yours, but as to a sale, the deceased's intention is quite clear. You may not sell it for tourist development. There are many conditions and clauses. Your great uncle was a great one for adding and subtracting.'

At this stage the lawyer preferred to keep his own counsel as to the legal loopholes of the will.

'St Christos must be kept as it is,' Alex broke in. 'No tourist development and . . . '

'And how do the people of the island see their future? I assume they're quite poor,' Martin countered.

'Depends how you define poor,' Alex said sharply. 'I believe . . . '

'You run a diving and fishing school?' Martin interrupted. 'Snorkelling, scuba, that sort of thing? So you don't see St Christos island as a possible extension of your own . . . er . . . business?'

'No, I do not. Gordon Ferguson and I were friends and we respected each other's views. He trusted me, and my job is to make sure his wishes are carried out to the letter.'

'No need to get heated, Mr Ross,' McGuire intervened. 'I'm sure Mr Ferguson saw you as a trusted friend, but if I may suggest, maybe there's some time for reflection at this stage. I believe you have a plane to catch this evening. I will, of course, keep you informed. You can see that your rôle is, in the main, accomplished. Miss Ferguson is a suitable legatee. She can take possession of her great uncle's estate at any time.'

'Provided she complies with the conditions.'

'Quite so, quite so. Agreed.'

The lawyer gathered up his papers.

'How long?' Alex asked abruptly.

'For as long as Miss Ferguson needs to consider all the possibilities, no doubt advised by family and fiancé.'

'The people of St Christos need a

swift decision. The island's grinding to a halt. It needs to see a future, a direction, a leader.'

'I don't see myself as an island leader,' Tessa said with a frown.

'Of course not.'

Jerry put his arm round her.

'Your life is with me and I don't intend we should spend it on some small, backwood island in the middle of nowhere. But we need time to think how best to dispose of this very unexpected legacy.'

'It is not disposable,' Alex almost shouted. 'Don't any of you see?'

He looked around the expensively-furnished library, its thick, brocaded curtains providing insulation from the busy London traffic below. They were all insulated from the reality of life on St Christos, the only life he considered real.

'Money doesn't come into it,' he continued quietly, already seeing the pound signs above Martin Carson's head.

Jerry Talbot he wasn't sure about. His face betrayed nothing but concern and love for Tessa.

Lucky guy, Alex thought, not for the first time. He went over to Tessa.

'I'll leave you to think it through. Mr McGuire has a letter for you from your great uncle. He showed it to me before he died. Please,' he lowered his voice, 'please, come to St Christos before you make any decision. Come and visit us. See for yourself.'

He took her hand, shook it briefly, then nodded to the others and left. Tessa felt the warm pressure again, saw his eyes, dark and troubled for the future of St Christos.

'Well,' McGuire said, 'that just about wraps it up for now.'

He handed Tessa a folder.

'The will, deeds of ownership. All the documents are there, plus your uncle's letter. Perhaps you'll ring me in a few days, just as soon as . . . er . . . what do you think of Mr Ross's suggestion, to visit the island?'

'Out of the question,' Margaret cut in. 'Tessa is getting married very soon and there's a great deal to do. I need her here so there'll be no time for island-gadding.'

Tessa took the papers from Douglas McGuire.

'Thanks. I'll be in touch soon.'

'If I can have a copy of the will,' Martin Carson said eagerly, 'I can get my legal team to run an eye over it. They're used to these rickety bequests drawn up by hick solicitors.'

'No, thank you, Martin. It's good of you to want to help but I don't really need your team just yet,' Tessa said, tucking the folder under her arm.

'I can help though,' Jerry said as he took her arm.

Margaret looked at Martin.

'Perhaps we should cancel dinner this evening and have a family conference.'

'Of course you must go out,' Tessa said. 'I know Jerry has a mountain of work tomorrow.'

'But . . . ' Jerry protested.

76

'No.' She kissed him. 'I'll ring you.'

'Promise you won't do anything without consulting me first.'

'Of course not. I'm really tired, and all this happening, too. So if you don't mind, I'll have an early night.'

She couldn't wait to be on her own, but once upstairs it seemed an age before the front door banged and the house was quiet.

An hour or so later, Tessa went downstairs and took a half bottle of Chablis from the fridge and held it to the light. Pure gold, pale but gold, like May sunshine. St Christos in May! She imagined the sun would be brighter there than in London, sparkling on a blue-green ocean. She sipped the wine and picked up her letter, trying to imagine the writer. An old man, white-haired? Tall? Sitting on the shaded veranda of his house looking towards green hills, or the azure sea surrounding his island? Her island!

Smoothing out the paper she read her great uncle's letter for the fourth time. It was precise. As Alex Ross had stated, sale for development other than to promote economic self-sufficiency amongst the islanders would nullify the legacy and Curtis Ollivière and Alex Ross would control the management in the same way Gordon Ferguson had done.

Tessa frowned. She knew little of the law but even she could see the provisos were frequently ambiguous and vague, but it was the final paragraph that tightened her fingers round the wine glass.

Because you are reading this, my beloved nephew, Jim, will be dead, but he lives on through you, Tessa Ferguson. You will have inherited his integrity. He was a great man. If only he had been my father, my life . . .

The words were blurred and smudged for the next few lines, a whole sentence crossed out then it went on.

I trust him implicitly and I trust you, dear, unknown niece, to act wisely for my island. Because you are Jim's daughter, I know you will not betray our trust. The island has magic which can bring you great joy, or sadness. That will be your choice.

Tessa shivered. There was no signature, merely the twined initials G.F. She took a huge gulp of wine and forced her memory back, to her father, loving and comforting, reading to her, taking her to the local primary school, explaining why Mummy couldn't take her. He was always there, or so it seemed. But, in the end, both betrayed her and sent her away to that awful school and then denied her the magic island escape. She never forgave them and it was Molly who became her friend and protector. Very soon after that her father died. Now tears mingled with her wine, tears of frustration and lost opportunities.

'Why, why didn't you tell me?' she cried out loud. 'It's all too late now.'

She folded the letter and pushed it crumpled into the envelope. They should have confided in her before. Her father should have taken her to the island. It had no magic now for her. She had her life here, and as Martin said, what did she want with a Caribbean island?

'You'll not disrupt my life now. I'm going to marry Jerry Talbot and be . . . '

'Tessa, are you all right? Who's in there with you?'

Molly opened the door.

'I've brought you a hot drink. Your mother told me. What a . . . a . . . '

'Shock? Surprise? All of those, I think, Molly, and please, come in and join me. I need to talk to you. Please, I want to talk to you about Dad.'

'Ah, well, I don't know. Och, your phone. All right, more wine, but are you sure? You must be tired. What about a hot drink?'

Tessa took the receiver.

'Oh, Jerry, hi. What a surprise tonight was, eh? No, I wasn't asleep. Still reeling, yes. I've read the letter and conditions. OK, later I'll have a lawyer.'

She pulled a face.

'No, not one of Martin's. I agree with

you there. No, I haven't made my mind up on anything. You said to wait . . . oh, all right then, tell me.'

She listened, nodded, sighed, while her fiancé talked.

Finally she said, 'Yes, you're probably right, Jerry. I will think about that. Now, here's Molly come to say good-night. We'll talk later. No, don't come round. Good-night.'

She put the phone down, and poured herself and Molly a glass of wine.

'A toast, Molly! It's not every day a girl's left a Caribbean island.'

'No indeed. So what do you intend . . . '

Tessa put her hand to her ears.

'Not you, too. I don't know! Let's just enjoy this extraordinary moment in our lives.'

She raised her glass.

'Here's to the future, whatever it is to be. Great Uncle Gordon writes I have a choice. Do I, Molly?'

'A good question, Tess. I don't know either but time will tell.'

But as Tessa drank to her future she

heard Jerry's voice, gentle, loving, persuasive.

'With that sort of money we really could make a difference, even a research fellowship. So much to be achieved.'

6

Tessa glanced at her watch as she hurried towards the main shopping centre. Less than two hours to polish off a yard-long list — swimsuits, sandals, evening casuals, underwear, and she had to book a facial, and definitely a new hairstyle. Maybe she should have heeded her mother's advice over breakfast that morning.

'You should take a few days off,' Margaret had urged, 'or you'll be a wreck on your wedding day. You look washed out. There's no necessity to kill yourself working, especially now.'

'I like work.'

'Oh, well,' Margaret had shrugged, 'your decision, but make sure you turn up this time for your wedding dress fitting on Friday. Kenneth's very busy. It was hard to fit you in.'

'The wedding's six weeks away. Plenty of time.'

'There isn't!' Margaret called out as the front door banged.

Guilt drove Tessa into the city's main shopping street in her shift break but her feet were soon aching as she passed department store after store, all their windows artistically merchandising autumn and winter wear. Summer was sliding away and the early September date set for her wedding was alarmingly close. The thick tweeds and full length coats were not suitable for the tropical island honeymoon Martin Carson had insisted on giving them.

Staring at the winter displays she saw the reflection of a figure standing directly behind her. She turned.

'Why, Alex Ross. I thought you were back on your island.'

'I was but I cleared a few things with James, my partner, and flew right back. I needed to check on my family in Scotland.'

'Such a surprise, coincidence, too. I

rarely come into town.'

She was absurdly pleased to see him.

Alex didn't tell her he'd followed her from the hospital where a busy nurse had told him, 'Tessa? Gone just this minute, honeymoon shopping. Probably Oxford Street, lucky woman. Jerry Talbot is such a catch.'

Alex smiled.

'I was lucky to see you then. There's a wine bar just along from here, or coffee?'

'I'm wedding shopping and beginning to think I've left it a bit late.'

'When's the wedding?'

'September.'

'Weeks yet,' he said and took her arm. 'I need to talk to you.'

She pulled away.

'It's impossible. Can't it wait?'

'No. It's important, Tessa. Please.'

'All right. Why not? I'm certainly not in the mood for shopping but I have to be back in a little over an hour.'

Alex steered her towards a side street and into a rather dingy wine bar. She peered into the gloomy interior.

'It's the nearest one, and quiet. I'll get drinks,' he suggested.

'Mineral water, please, I'm working.'

He went to the bar and as Tessa's eyes adjusted she saw they were the only customers and it was more intimate than gloomy. Alex's broad figure seemed even larger in the diminutive bar and, by the set of his shoulders, she knew he was more at home outdoors than in. He brought the drinks back to the table.

'Thanks,' she said and couldn't help smiling.

'What?'

'That stool, this room. It's too small for you. You look uncomfortable.'

'I feel it. I'm used to more space around me, though it wasn't always so. I used to feel completely at home in London but after St Marques and St Christos, well, it's claustrophobic.'

'So why did you come back?'

'I can't settle until we have a decision on St Christos. The people are uneasy.

No work's being done, crops are neglected, the young men talk of leaving the island and finding work in St Vincent or Barbados. Uncertainty, rumour about development, the new owner . . . '

'Wouldn't development bring jobs to the island?'

'Maybe, but before Gordon died nobody even considered leaving. The people were happy.'

Tessa frowned.

'How can you be so sure? From the information you gave me there's little in the way of modern amenities, no hospital, no regular schooling. It seems to me to be a century behind.'

'You're judging by Western standards. Just because there are no supermarkets, no cinemas or fast-food outlets, you seem to think it's uncivilised. Don't you ever consider how uncivilised our lifestyles are now? Frantic pace, no time to stop and stare — you've looked at your watch at least four times since we've been here. Your mind's on the wards and not in the slightest concerned with St Christos or its people.'

'That's not fair. I have thought about it — of them — constantly. I've tried hard to imagine what it's like but . . . '

She stopped herself in the nick of time from glancing at her watch.

'If that were true you'd have been over to the island within days.'

'It's only two weeks since I learned of the legacy. I do have a life to lead here and I'm getting married in less than six weeks. I didn't realise it had to be an instant decision. I can't just drop everything and swan off to some Caribbean island.'

'Is that how you see the legacy your great uncle left — some Caribbean island?'

They glared at each other, Tessa's face flushed with anger, tiredness and tension, clouding reason.

'Yes, I do see it like that. I didn't ask him to leave me the place. He and my dad were just impractical dreamers and now they've foisted this burden on me. I do not want it and I'd be grateful to anyone who'd take it off my hands, at a knock-down price if necessary, and as for you coming all this way just to harass me . . . '

She stopped and bit her lip. Alex's face was dark, his blue eyes hardened in anger.

'I . . . I'm sorry.' She wished she could swallow the words. 'I didn't mean . . . '

'It's clear you did mean it. You have no interest in St Christos and apparently no family loyalty either. Gordon would have been deeply disappointed.'

She leaned forward.

'Look, I really am sorry. I'm tired, there's a lot on my mind, but believe me I haven't forgotten St Christos at all. It's just . . . '

She hesitated. Both Jerry and Martin had urged her not to communicate with Alex Ross. Neither of them trusted him and both maintained he had his own reasons for wanting the island not to be sold, commercial reasons. But it wasn't fair to keep the information from him.

'I suppose I shouldn't tell you,' she said slowly, 'but Martin's legal friends got hold of a copy of the will. Don't ask me how. I was furious but evidently McGuire's father drew up the will when he was well past it and apparently there are so many holes in the wording of the conditions they're more or less nullified. As his lawyer friends see it, the island is mine with no strings.'

She put her hand out to reach his but he drew back and stared at her.

'Yes,' he said, 'that's exactly what I was afraid of. McGuire hinted as much when I phoned last week.'

'Your St Christos lawyer can't be very good. He should have known better. Why didn't he check out the London firm?'

Alex shrugged.

'Curtis is a good guy but the whole ethos over there is different. According to Curtis once Gordon's wishes were known, they couldn't be clearer. He trusted everyone to take it as read.'

'That's a bit unworldly.'

'And stupid, go on say it. You can't imagine anyone could be so trusting, especially when there's money to be made.'

He stood up.

'I'm sorry for you, Tessa. I reckoned you were different but you're ready to sell your own soul like all the rest. Now you'll never know the magic of St Christos. Maybe you'll visit some day, stay at an exclusive resort for the seriously rich. Oh, it'll be beautifully manicured and civilised luxury, very desirable, very expensive, but it will have lost its soul and that is a great tragedy. I wish you joy for your life here.'

He moved so quickly he'd merged into the gloom before she could reply.

'Alex, come back, I haven't said . . . '

The barman looked across at her.

'He's out of the door, miss. Moved like lightning.'

She picked up her bag, saw the time

and gasped. She'd be late unless she could grab a taxi. As she ran out into the bright sunlight she realised she hadn't looked at her watch once since Alex had mentioned it.

The ward was frantically busy when Tessa got back. She was late home and had a date with Jerry in the evening so it wasn't until next morning at work she snatched a rare quiet moment to phone Douglas McGuire.

'I need to contact Alex Ross. Do you know where he is staying?'

'He's flying back to the Caribbean tonight. Business or something. Nothing more he could do here,' he said. 'Apparently you told him about the will. It is worse than a colander, full of legal holes but to your benefit. You can proceed with the sale of St Christos as soon as probate is cleared.'

'Yes, I told him. I thought it unfair not to.'

'No great harm now. I suspect he knew all along. He's no fool, although Curtis Ollivière could do with brushing up his inheritance skills.'

'But wasn't it your father in the first place and then ultimately your responsibility to see great uncle's wishes are carried out?'

'My dear, the burden rests on your shoulders. We are merely your . . . er . . . employees. On the one hand you can sell St Christos. I have an offer on the table already from Toplan Leisure-world. Very keen purchasers. On the other hand you can struggle on as . . . um . . . queen of St Christos but I would warn you that you would need to spend a considerable amount of time and probably a good deal of money there to make it a viable project.'

'Why couldn't I just find a manager?'

There was a barely concealed snort of derision.

'Be an absentee landlord with all the trouble that usually entails, or a solid proposition from Toplan? I know which I'd choose.'

Tessa saw Sister Bedford signalling frantically from the end of the ward.

'I've got to go. I'll phone again later.'

Guiltily she put the phone down and hurried to her patient.

In his office, Douglas McGuire shook his head in part amazement, part amusement. Why on earth did the girl go on working when there was a fortune just waiting to be picked up and, incidentally, a nice little percentage of that for himself if all went to plan? He dialled his old friend Harry Toplan's personal number.

Tessa had arranged to meet her mother for a dress fitting late that afternoon and just about had time to dash home, change out of her uniform and grab a cup of tea.

'There's a message on your answerphone,' Molly called out from downstairs. 'Sounds like that nice young man who came along with the lawyer. Alex, isn't it? And your ma said after the fitting you and she are meeting Jerry for a drink.'

'OK, thanks.'

Tessa switched on the machine and

started to unbutton her uniform. Her fingers stilled as Alex's voice with its faint Scottish lilt filled the room.

'Tessa, I'm flying back tonight. There's nothing to be done here. I talked to McGuire and he says St Christos is already on the market. If that's what you want, good luck. Anyway, I'm sorry I blew up yesterday. I'd no right, and I'd rather we stayed friends, maybe in different circumstances. Come and see the island before it changes, before it loses its magic. You owe it to yourself and to us. You'll regret it if you don't. Please come, Tessa.'

The message ended abruptly. Tessa stared out over the treetops of the London square. Alex's voice had rekindled her dream, promised that magic was still out there. Tessa snapped out of her reverie and ran downstairs and off to the dress fitting.

'It's magnificent, Kenneth, superb. Doesn't she look a dream?' Tessa's mother suffused.

Kenneth nodded, puffed with pride

at his achievement. Tessa wasn't so sure. She felt imprisoned by yards of billowing silk train, and while the cream satin dress was beautifully cut there was too much fancy work for her taste.

'Don't you think it's a bit over the top, Mother? My style is, well, plainer. These sleeves are enormous, too puffed.'

'They can easily be altered.'

Kenneth dashed forward, pin cushion at the ready.

'But you want to stand out from everybody on your wedding day,' her mother persisted.

'I'll easily do that. There'll be no room for anyone else in the church with all this material. I'm sure the original design was much simpler.'

'You missed the last two appointments so Kenneth and I had to improvise.'

Tessa picked up the train.

'I'll tell you what. Clip a few yards off the train. Why do I need a train anyway? Make the sleeves a closer fit, and short. And cheer up, Mother, I'm sure you'll outshine me anyway. You're always the star attraction.'

Margaret gave her a sharp look.

'Is that how you see me? You really think I want to outshine you on your wedding day?'

'No, but . . . don't look like that. I didn't mean anything but you've always been a woman of style and beauty. I can't compete and I don't want to. I'm proud of you.'

She took off the dress.

'Phew, that's better. Thanks, Kenneth. A few little . . . um . . . alterations? Down-size it a bit?'

He gave her a conspiratorial wink.

'No problem. Next week, same time?'

'Er, probably not.'

Tessa glanced at her mother who for once was silent.

'Ring me then when you're sure. There's not much time left. You'll be a picture,' he told her as he ushered them out.

They met Jerry in the roof-top bar of an expensive hotel. He kissed Tessa, then Margaret.

'I've ordered champagne. Over there.'

He indicated a table by the huge, plate-glass window.

'There you are, Tess, top of the world, and that's where we're going. Everything's ahead of us. How did the fitting go? Dress OK?'

'A bit over the top but I've toned it down. I hope Kenneth took note.'

Jerry frowned.

'Why do you always undersell yourself? You keep doing it. I'll take you shopping after we're married.'

Tessa was startled. It was difficult to imagine Jerry in a woman's clothes shop, but then there were lots of things she didn't know about him.

'Fortunately I can't see you finding time for that. Anyway I do prefer to shop for myself.'

She smiled at him but he didn't return it. There was a small silence before he raised his glass.

'To us, Tessa, and our future. I guarantee it'll be a golden one.'

She drank and felt the bubbles of

oxygen race in her blood. She carefully put down her glass.

'Jerry, you know I have some time off before the wedding, at least two weeks.'

'You'll need them, according to Margaret. Shopping, fittings . . . '

'No, I can sort those out later. I want to go to St Christos before the wedding.'

'St Christos? What for? You've decided to sell it.'

'No, no, I haven't, not yet. You've all decided I'm going to sell it. I'd like to see it first before I decide.'

Jerry and Margaret exchanged glances.

'I don't think that's a good idea,' Margaret said.

'Not practical,' Jerry added.

'Why not? I have the time and it's criminal not to see Great Uncle Gordon's island before it's spoiled. Jerry, you could come with me, a sort of pre-honeymoon.'

'Out of the question,' he said in a cool tone. 'I have a conference I have to prepare for along with a long list of private patients. Impossible.'

'But don't you want to see St Christos?'

'I've seen it,' he burst out angrily.

'You've seen it. How?'

Tessa's heart beat faster.

'A . . . a friend, a patient of mine, holidaying in the Caribbean, took an aerial video of some of the smaller islands. He pointed out St Christos to me, that's all.'

'Why didn't you tell me, show me the video?'

'I forgot. I meant to,' he replied and looked away, embarrassed, and for the first time Tessa saw her fiancé discomfited.

She realised that he'd never meant to tell her. She looked at him steadily.

'Well, I'm going. You could come with me.'

'You know you're asking the impossible. Have you been in touch with Alex Ross? He's put this absurd notion into your head.'

'What if he has? I should have had

the guts to go right away. I want to see my island and I'm going to book a flight right away.'

Jerry stood up. Tessa thought how immaculately handsome he looked at the end of a busy working day. She smiled at him.

'Please come, Jerry. It'd be fun.'

'I'm disappointed in you, Tessa,' he said. 'Have you any idea just how childish you're being? I'll ring you in the morning when you're possibly more sensible. Margaret, good-night.'

His nod towards Tessa was a mere token of politeness.

'Well,' Margaret said as she picked up her glass, 'you've done it now. Jerry has a very stubborn streak.'

'I don't care. I'm going to St Christos and Jerry will just have to accept it. I'll try Helen if you or Jerry won't come.'

Suddenly she was desperate to book a flight and to be on the way to her magic island just to see, she told herself, if it really was magic, as Alex had promised.

7

Tessa, how wonderful! How terrible!'
Helen enthused. 'I do have the weekend
free but my sister's about to produce
nephew number three. I promised to
help out. I would have loved to come to
St Christos. I can't bear to think about
it. Imagine, wet Wales with those two
roaring boys or the sunny Caribbean
with you. No contest normally but I did
promise.'

Tessa hid her disappointment.

'I'm not sure why Jerry's so set
against it. But anyway, I'm going. I'll
find a flight, but I thought I'd check
you out first.'

Helen pulled a face as she said, 'Ring
me the minute you get back. Make me
really green.'

'I hope I shall. See you soon.'

Tessa managed to get a late flight
cancellation at the end of the week. Her

stint in obstetrics ended Wednesday, with a week before she went back to her favourite paediatrics. She booked the flight and faxed Alex her arrival time in Barbados. She was about to start packing when Jerry rang.

'Tessa,' he said, his voice warm, apologetic, 'I'm sorry about walking out on you and Margaret at the restaurant.'

'That's OK. We're all a bit on edge, I expect.'

'It was the thought of you going away without me, especially to a tropical island. That was to be for us, on honeymoon.'

She closed her eyes, imagining their honeymoon, but spoke firmly.

'You could still come with me. I've booked my flight, Friday.'

'Darling, I'd love to come and I've tried to rearrange my schedule but it's impossible. I shall just have to concentrate on our wedding. Not long now.'

'I'm sorry, Jerry, but you do see . . .'

'Of course. I was just being selfish. Forgive me. I'll take you to the airport.

I'm free Friday morning.'

'You're forgiven, and I'd like that. Ten o'clock Friday, from Heathrow.'

'I'll pick you up at the house, and, Tessa, remember, I love you.'

'I love you, too.'

She wished he could come with her and even more so when he picked her up Friday morning. In casual chinos and dark open-neck shirt he looked too attractive to leave behind. The traffic was horrendous and they hit a jam just before Heathrow. The plane was on time and already boarding when they arrived.

'Thanks, Jerry, it was sweet of you to see me off. Shame it's such a rush,' Tessa said sincerely.

'Time to give you these, as an apology for the other evening.'

The black pearl earrings were a perfect match for her engagement ring.

'Jerry, they're beautiful.'

'Shall I keep them for you?'

'I suppose that's safest,' she said and handed them back reluctantly.

'And it's insurance for me. You'll have to come back now, to claim your earrings and me.'

'There's no doubt about that,' Tessa said. 'It's only a few days but I'll miss you.'

'It'll soon pass and I'll meet you. I've got your plane times.'

With a final wave, he left her and she watched his tall figure thread confidently through the crowds until he was out of sight.

When the plane landed in Barbados it was morning and a different world, hot and humid. Alex Ross, smiling and waving, met her.

'You got here!'

He picked her up, swung her round and round and ended in a bear hug which threatened to knock the air from her lungs.

'Hey,' she managed to grunt, 'you'll crush me to death before I get to St Christos.'

He put her down and they stood awkwardly for a moment. Alex wore very short shorts and a brief T-shirt. His tan was even more marked than in London, his hair seemed longer and it was more tousled.

'I'm sorry,' he repeated, 'it's just . . . I never really believed you'd get here. Even after your fax I expected a message every minute to say you'd changed your mind. Come on, my plane's parked farther along.'

'Your plane?'

'Sure. How else do we hop from island to island? I'll take your bag. My, you're a light traveller.'

'In this heat, I shan't need much to wear.'

'Too true. It's not far to the outer runway. We'll hop over to St Marques tonight if that's all right. James, my cousin, would like to meet you, and I'd like you to see St Christos in daylight. We'll take a boat in the morning.'

'Fine.'

She was disappointed but it made sense.

'Here we are. There are two more passengers.'

A young couple, hands entwined, got up from a wooden bench to greet Alex. The girl put her arms round his neck and kissed him.

'Great to be back again.'

'Hi, Jeannie, Mark. This is Tessa Ferguson from London. She's going to St Christos tomorrow. Tessa, Mark and Jeannie are on a diving holiday.'

'Our fourth one,' Jeannie said. 'We love it, but this one's kind of special. We're getting married on St Marques next Saturday. I hope you'll still be here and come along.'

Her wide smile was warm and friendly, her arms tightly linked with her husband-to-be.

The tiny, eight-seater plane took off with as much flourish as a jumbo jet from Heathrow. Tessa clung tightly to her seat as the plane lurched into the air, but she soon got used to the sensation and it seemed no time at all until Alex pointed downwards.

'St Marques. See the airfield to the right?'

They began to descend to what looked like a billiard table of green turf where Alex landed his plane smoothly. The smart, new airport terminal was deserted except for a couple of smiling guards who doubled up as customs officers, and a tall blond man who rushed forward to meet them.

'Alex, Mark and Jeannie, good to see you all, and you have to be Tessa Ferguson. I'm really glad to see you, Tessa. We're letting you down gently today. I've booked you a room at a small hotel bang on the ocean. We'll join you for dinner if you're not too tired.'

'No, I'm not. Sounds great.'

'Peach and Quiet, the hotel you're going to, takes our overflow. Our guest accommodation's a bit basic.'

'I wouldn't mind that.'

'Peach and Quiet's better and in any case we've had an out-of-the-blue booking from a London diving club. A long weekend would you believe? So we're stacked out.'

'If I can get a word in,' Alex said, 'this is James, or Jim, my cousin and partner.'

Tessa smiled.

'I assumed that.'

She liked James immediately and although he was blond and brown-eyed, the very opposite of Alex's colouring, there was an unmistakeable family likeness.

She'd protested she wasn't tired but the rest of the day took on a dreamlike air that could only have been the result of jet lag. The details blurred. There was a warm welcome from the St Marques owners of Peach and Quiet, a spacious, comfortable room, a siesta, then Alex and James with Jeannie and Mark in tow turned up for dinner.

Alex didn't say much. James did most of the talking, first of London, then of St Marques' diving and the best snorkelling places, and it was Alex who eventually brought the evening to an end.

'I guess we should all go to bed. Early start tomorrow. I'll pick you up about eight, Tessa. Sleep well.'

'I shall,' she promised.

The breeze was fresh next day, the waves white-capped. It was an exhilarating sail from St Marques but Tessa's heart began to thump as St Christos's land mass grew larger. Soon they were running only feet away from a sheer cliff face. It looked forbidding, high enough to darken the sun. Alex caught her anxious look.

'This is Christos's inhospitable side, impossible to land anywhere here. I thought I'd show you the worst first. Wait until we round that point.'

He slewed the boat round the western point of the island where the cliffs were not so high and were covered in lush greenery. Rocky inlets gave glimpses of small, palm-fringed beaches of pure white sand and turquoise water. Alex reduced speed to navigate treacherous-looking rocks ringing a series of small landing stages.

'Whoever are all these people up there?' Tessa asked apprehensively.

'It's the welcoming party. Practically everyone on the island, I'd say. They've all turned out to meet you, Gordon's great-niece.'

'Goodness, I'm glad I didn't know about this. I would've caught the next plane home. What shall I do?'

'Be yourself. They just want to have a look at you and say hello and welcome.'

He threw a rope on to the jetty which was swiftly caught by willing hands and after a slight hesitation Tessa took her first steps on to the island, Alex close behind her.

The crowd fell silent. Dark brown faces eyed her intently, then an old man stepped forward and took her hand.

'Welcome, Gordon's great-niece. I am chief elder of St Christos. We are happy to welcome you here and wish you all the happiness of St Christos.'

He motioned forward a small, dark-eyed girl who reached up and shyly placed a garland of flowers around Tessa's neck.

'Thank you, thank you all . . . er . . . I

am very happy to be here, to see my great uncle's island. I am honoured by your welcome.'

Approving applause rippled round the crowd then all of a sudden, and by common consent, they melted away, some smiling at her, some waving. Within two minutes the landing stage was deserted.

'How very extraordinary.'

'Not really. They're giving you space, privacy, but someone will be watching your every move. You look totally stunned. Let's get you up to Bella's. She's got breakfast for us. Curtis will be in the yard.'

'The lawyer?'

He nodded.

'Taxi driver as well when business is slow, which it frequently is. He was a good friend of Gordon's and a friend of mine, too.'

'Not much of a lawyer, though,' Tessa couldn't help adding.

'That's not really fair. He drew up the very simple original will but in his later years Gordon became paranoid about the future. That's why your father's visit gave the ideal solution. His mistake was to go to London lawyers. That complicated things as we've seen, and look, there's Curtis.'

'Miss Tessa, at last!'

Curtis Ollivière pumped both her hands up and down.

'Been waiting here for hours in case I missed you. Step aboard.'

The taxi was like a small, open-air truck with wooden seats on either side. A canvas canopy gave shelter from sun and showers and its support provided hand holds for the passengers.

'Do you want to ride up front with me?' Curtis asked.

'No, this is wonderful. A perfect way to see the island.'

Alex nodded approvingly and clambered alongside her.

'Most of the transport's like this, or scooters.'

Tessa clung to the wooden strut as the taxi shot forward. The road from the harbour was quite good but soon gave way to a dirt road which wound steadily upwards through coconut groves, banks of bougainvillea, and exotic shrubs she didn't recognise. Occasionally the vegetation would thin giving glimpses of glittering ocean below. They dropped down a steep hill, turned a sharp corner and the whole bay lay spread before them.

'Wow!' Tessa exclaimed. 'What a view.'

Curtis turned into a lane.

'That's the view from Gordon's veranda. He spent most of his last days there, looking out to sea.'

He brought the taxi to a halt by a long, low building surrounded by a wooden deck.

'And there's Bella, waiting for us, since dawn, I bet. She looked after Gordon for many years and now she's lost without him.'

A white-haired, plump, dark-eyed, middle-aged woman with a wide, friendly smile came forward.

'At last!' she echoed Curtis's greeting

but put out her arms to Tessa who just naturally went into them.

Bella held her close for a few seconds before releasing her.

'My, my I can just see your father there. Can't you, Curtis?'

'My father?'

Tessa hadn't thought of him actually being there.

'You knew him?'

'Of course I did. Didn't he stay here in this house with his uncle all of his time at Christos? And sorry we were to see him go. He promised he would bring you next visit, but we never heard another word.'

'He died, when I was ten.'

'Aw, no. Well, I suspected as much. Gordon wouldn't have it though, kept saying he was bound to turn up just like before, then as the years went on it all faded away. Why didn't you write to tell us your father had died?'

'I . . . we never knew about Uncle Gordon, or St Christos.'

Bella shook her head.

'That's so strange, but come on in, come in. I just hope you're all hungry. There's breakfast on the table, St Christos style.'

Tessa realised she was ravenously hungry, and couldn't remember when she'd last had that sensation. The table was set by a wide-screened window opening on to the deck. The ocean view was breathtaking. Green hills cradled the turquoise bay where a couple of fishing boats bobbed lazily.

'It's so beautiful.'

She couldn't tear herself away from the deck.

'Eat first, plenty of time to sit and rock on the deck later. I want to hear all about London.'

Bella piled food on to plates — eggs, some kind of smoked meat, rice dishes smelling of nutmeg, mace and some indefinable spice, piles of fruit and dark, home-made bread.

'Alex, you'll be showing Tessa around the island after breakfast?'

'I can't, Bella. I was hoping Curtis, or

116

you, could do a tour. We've an influx of visitors and I've got to get back to give James a hand, but it's only a weekend package so I'll be free after that. Maybe you'd like a day's snorkelling around St Marques, Tessa. Curtis could bring you over.'

'I'd like that. This food is great. I shall get very fat if all your meals are like this, Bella.'

'They will be. Anyway you're too thin. I shall feed you up. How long do you stay?'

'Just under a week. I leave Thursday.'

'No! That's not enough. Alex, tell her.'

'Not my business. Tessa is a working woman and she's getting married in six weeks.'

'Married? But who? How? You are returning to St Christos though, with your husband perhaps?'

'I don't think . . . Please, can I just be here for a while? I'm not sure.'

'Sure, I'm sorry. It's just we've waited so long and now . . . those men are here again,' Bella said.

'What men?' Curtis and Alex said together.

Bella rolled her eyes.

'The men in white suits, three of them this time.'

'How did they come? Who brought them?' Alex asked.

'A very smart yacht, moored off Devil's Point. Someone rowed them to the jetty.'

Alex turned to Curtis.

'Do you know anything about them?'

'No, I've been away on a fishing trip. I did hear there's a couple staying at Janie's, our only guest house,' he explained to Tessa. 'She opened up 'specially. I did hear they had visitors, maybe the men in suits. I'll ask around.'

Bella poured more coffee, her lips pursed.

'Perhaps I shouldn't mention it right now but my nephew, Joseph, on the other side of the island, has heard rumours of a helicopter pad being built.'

'That is impossible,' Alex said. 'The island belongs to Tessa. They'd need her permission which I hope she wouldn't give. Besides it's too hilly that side.'

Bella shrugged.

'Anything's possible if there's cash in it, and we don't go in much for planning applications here. Gordon was our planning officer and there was no-one else to ask.'

She looked meaningfully at Tessa.

'Until now,' she added.

'It just wasn't possible to come to St Christos earlier. These things take time to arrange.'

Even to Tessa's own ears it sounded feeble. Now she was on the island it seemed the most natural place to be.

'But I should have realised. I was so busy.'

'I know how it is,' Bella said sympathetically, 'but the islanders are getting restless, especially the young people. They're going over to Barbados instead of working our own fields and in the town they get a better standard of living, cinemas, hotels, clubs. They come back discontented, talking of good jobs in Barbados hotels and bars. You know, all of Gordon's teaching, to love what's natural, what we have here, it'll soon be forgotten.'

She put a hand over Tessa's.

'We'd like to know what's going to happen to our island and you're the only one who can tell us.'

'I wish I knew,' Tessa replied quietly, 'I really do, but I promise I will make a decision now I'm here. After all, that's what I've come for.'

8

Bella was obviously delighted to be the St Christos official tour guide for Tessa.

'I'll clear breakfast and we'll be away,' she said after Alex and Curtis had left. 'I have the truck so we can see the whole island. I was chauffeur and housekeeper to your great uncle. He was the pleasure of my life,' she added simply. 'I'll see to the dishes. You just look round the house and garden. It's lovely to have you here. It's been lonely since Gordon died.'

'I'm very glad to be here.'

Tessa wandered through the house. Apart from the main living area the rooms were small, sparsely furnished. In a tiny den hardly bigger than a cupboard she found shelves crammed with books and a few photographs on a top shelf. She recognised one of her family, Margaret, her father and herself, a little girl. She picked it up. Margaret looked cross, her father sad and ill, and herself anxious-looking. It was not a happy picture.

'There are better ones of your family,' Bella said as she came into the study, 'but that was Gordon's favourite. I don't know why. He and your father got on so well. Your dad loved St Christos and I believe he meant to settle here eventually. I hope you may feel the same once you've seen our island. Are you ready for me to show it to you?'

The one good road circled the island running alongside the spice fields and banana plantations. Everywhere they went Tessa was the focus of interest and attention. Most people called out a greeting, children waved. An atmosphere of friendly tranquillity pervaded the island, its beauty surrounding them on all sides.

Once Bella left the main track to push the protesting vehicle up a narrow, winding path into the tropical rain forest in the centre of the island, it was breathtaking and all too soon she bumped them back on to the road.

'Now for the town, our commercial centre,' she said proudly.

The town, incongruously named Dumfries, was behind the main jetties and boasted a post office, bank, pharmacy, several stores and a garage. A fruit and vegetable market was a central focus in an open square. Again everyone stopped trading to wave and smile.

'They all know who you are.'

Bella parked the truck by the jetties and they were soon walking the dusty streets.

'Library, school,' Bella indicated. 'Gordon was very keen on education. Let's go in.'

The school was a concrete rectangle with mesh screens over the windows. Small children sat around low tables colouring picture books or making clay models. Older children squatted on the ground, listening to stories or reading to older women.

'Our women take turns helping the children read and write, the men take them fishing or out in the fields to tend the crops.'

'Is there no qualified teacher?'

'No, but the children learn, as you see.'

Tessa stayed silent. It looked shapeless and chaotic but the children seemed happy enough and soon started to leave their groups to talk to her. Gradually they all came out, keen to hear about England, especially London. A helper brought out juice and biscuits and the afternoon lessons turned into a happy picnic, all eager to hear more about Tessa's own 'island'.

'Well,' Bella said when they at last managed to leave the premises, 'at least they had a geography lesson today.'

'They didn't seem at all sure where England was.'

'Would you have known where St Christos was at their ages?'

'That's different.'

'Not really. St Christos is their world, London's yours. Gordon taught that we have a much better quality of life here.'

'You're probably right,' she said tactfully.

'I know I am, but now you deserve a reward and I'm going to take you to my secret beach for a swim.'

'That sounds like paradise, too. The day's gone so quickly. I've loved it, and the island. Thank you, Bella.'

Impulsively she leaned over and hugged her.

'Ah! My great pleasure, far too long delayed.'

Bella's secret beach was indeed pure paradise, a secluded palm-fringed cove with soft very pale pink sand and a warm blue-green sea. The water was crystal clear and Tessa could have stayed there until the end of time, but as the sun began to go down Bella gathered up the towels and mats and drove back to the house.

Each day on St Christos was perfect. The morning after Tessa's introduction to the island Curtis took her on his boat to St Marques for a session with the Ross cousins' diving school. It was fun to be with a group of people who were determined to exact maximum enjoyment from their long weekend of water sports in the Caribbean. Alex and James supervised scuba diving whilst Tessa soaked up sunshine on deck.

'Take care you don't burn,' Alex warned her.

He saw a different creature from the harassed young woman who'd crashed into him in London.

'You look more relaxed and . . . '

A shout from James brought him to his feet.

'After the dive, there's a beach barbecue then I'm free for a few hours. Would you like to snorkel off the reef after lunch?'

'I should really get back to St Christos. That's really why I'm here, to understand the island.'

'And its neighbours. Don't worry, I'll get you back in good time.'

'All right then, I'd like that.'

Tessa rolled over on to her stomach, a soft warm breeze shivering over her skin as she relaxed in the sun. She couldn't help the holiday feeling, after all it was years since she'd had a real holiday and there were plenty of days left to think about the future.

Later in the day, she and Alex swam and snorkelled round one of the many reefs near the island. The kaleidoscope of swirling shapes and colours was fascinating and as a particularly brilliantly-striped fish swam beneath her she turned to see if Alex had noticed it. He was closer than she realised. They collided and her mouth-piece fell off. Choking with sea water she struggled for breath but Alex caught her and held her clear of the water.

'Sorry,' she gasped, 'so stupid, so beautiful.'

He laughed.

'Don't worry, take a breath.'

He still held her as the silken water

washed them closer together.

'I'm fine,' she said slowly.

He let her go and she adjusted her mask and mouthpiece and turned back to the water which seemed warmer than ever.

As the days passed, Tessa immersed herself more and more in the affairs of the island. She revisited the spice fields and banana plantations and went some way inland to the market gardens supplying fruit and vegetables to the islands. She met several of the elders, the wise old men who supervised all the aspects of St Christos life as laid down by Gordon decades ago.

Everywhere she met the same story — what did she intend to do about St Christos? Could she not see that work had slowed down? They needed a decision. Why could she not give one yet?

The afternoons Curtis went fishing he would drop her off at St Marques and she would join in with whatever was going on at the diving school or simply sit on the beach and watch the fishermen. It was quiet when the weekenders left, and she got to know Jeannie and Mark who were planning to settle on St Marques after their wedding.

'You must stay,' Jeannie pleaded. 'We want you as a witness.'

'My plane's on Thursday.'

'You can change that. Do you have to be at work then?'

'Well, no, but I'm . . . '

London, the wedding, all seemed like happenings on a distant planet. She'd spoken to Jerry once since she'd arrived. He was going to the States, an emergency, filling in for a colleague. He sounded excited. The wedding wasn't mentioned and he avoided any mention of the island. But St Christos held her enthralled and she wasn't ready to let it go just yet. She phoned the airline — no problem, there were seats available on Saturday week. So the daily routine continued, to Bella's great delight.

The day before Jeannie's and Mark's wedding, Alex sailed over to St Christos. He'd promised to take her to Gordon's grave, the only place Bella hadn't shown her.

'I go on my own. I'm not ready to share it yet,' she'd said. 'Best Alex takes you. Later we'll go together.'

Bella refused to believe Tessa wouldn't be part of the island's future although Tessa had told her over and over that she had to go back.

'Yes, yes, so you say. Work, marry perhaps, but you will come back to St Christos. I know it here.' She touched her heart. 'You can't avoid it.'

The boy from the post office arrived on his bike seconds before Alex.

'Fax for Miss Tessa Ferguson,' he announced importantly. 'Miss Adèle mislaid it. Sorry, not my fault. They want you back in London urgently.'

'Who does?' but the boy was out of the door and speeding down the lane before he got the blame for the delay, and reading someone else's mail!

'What is it? Bad news?' Bella asked.

'My mother wants me back right away. In fact this is dated the day after I arrived. Oh, dear.'

'A problem?' Alex asked as he arrived on the scene. 'She's not ill?'

'Mother? She's never ill. No, there's a meeting at McGuire's the lawyers. They need me there. She doesn't say why.'

'I can guess.'

Alex's voice was carefully expressionless.

'The meeting was last Saturday anyway. Ridiculous to have expected me to go straight back. I'll phone tomorrow.'

The nearest telephone was at the post office. In his later years, with typically eccentricity, Gordon had had the telephone at the house taken out.

'Are we walking to the grave, Alex?' she asked.

'If you want to. It's not far but the track's a bit rough.'

They walked down to the town and out up the hill past the white wood

131

church. Alex paused a moment.

'That's where we held Gordon's funeral service. Quite a day. There was a rainstorm, then sunshine for the burial, just as he would have wanted it.'

The cliff path rose steeply to the burial place. He turned and held out his hand. He pulled her up beside him and kept hold of her hand as they reached the graveside.

A simple headstone was inscribed: **Gordon Cameron Ferguson born Dumfries, Scotland. Died St Christos, aged about 99 years. Our leader and our teacher. He will be missed**.

Tessa kneeled and put a posy of flowers picked from the garden of his house on his grave. They stood in silence for a while then Alex spoke.

'What will you do, Tessa?'

'I don't know, I truly don't. Oh, I can see why you love this place, the lifestyle, the peace but somehow it's not real. It, or Gordon, pushed out the real world and you'll have to let it in sometime. Bella said the young are already drifting away. I can't run the island, you must see that.'

'I do, but Gordon at least hoped you'd try and keep things as they are.'

'From the other side of the world?'

'There are ways.'

She closed her eyes.

'Please, not now. I've still nearly a week left. Tell me about my great uncle. You knew him really well?'

He sighed.

'It'd take more time than you've got to tell you about Gordon Ferguson.'

'Tell me the important bits then.'

'All right, I'll try. There's a bench over there facing the sea. To quote Gordon, he didn't want people to gawp at a pile of mud and old bones when they could sit at the ocean and think about him there.'

Obediently they sat for a while admiring the magnificent sweep of ocean where golden light was turning to faint pink. The air was still warm, and their bare arms touched as Alex began Gordon's story.

'I met Gordon when I came here with my father. He, my dad, was an importer of spices, bananas, all things tropical. I was ten or eleven on my first visit.'

'Why, that's when I should have come with my father, Gordon's nephew. How strange.'

'It is. I may have met your father, I can't recall. I was usually sent out to play in his wonderful magic garden.'

'Magic?'

'He said it was. All his plants and flowers had healing powers. He strongly believed in natural cures. Anyway, I loved it, garden and island, and as trade prospered with my father we came more often and later I came on my own, but that's my story, not Gordon's.'

'I'd like to hear yours, too.'

'Would you?'

Their eyes met, sparked, then slid away back to the ocean.

'Another time,' he murmured. 'Gradually I learned more about Gordon. Born around the turn of the century in Scotland, he was destined for great things, an engineer, the family golden boy. Then there was some scandal, an older married woman, a minister's wife — an affair. Worst of all, she became pregnant, a dreadful sin as you can imagine, especially as she killed herself rather than face things. Apparently the local and national Press was full of it. Gordon, the culprit, was pilloried so he ran away to sea. He was only seventeen.

'Three years later he was ship-wrecked on St Christos and when the rest of the crew was rescued he stayed on, developed an island trade in spices and bananas and married a local girl, Celeste. She was three months pregnant when news came from Scotland that his mother was dying and wanted to see him. It was Celeste apparently who persuaded him to go and to take her with him.'

'She actually wanted to leave St Christos? According to Bella no-one ever did back then.'

'Well, not for good, but Celeste, according to Gordon, was a rare woman. She wanted to see the world and Scotland was a good place to start. Quite a trip in those days. Gordon rationalised that a sea voyage would be good for a mother-to-be.'

Alex picked up a stone and threw it over the cliff.

'So?' Tessa prompted, visualising the eager young Scot and his bride.

'So, when they arrived home, Gordon's mother was very ill. It was pneumonia and in spite of Gordon's objections, Celeste insisted on nursing Mrs Ferguson herself. Unfortunately, she contracted the disease. It was winter and damp. She died and the baby, a boy, was stillborn an hour later.'

'How dreadful. That's so terrible.'

'Gordon always blamed himself for taking her away from St Christos. The climate of his homeland killed both her and possibly the child.'

'Is that why Gordon had no faith in

modern medicine?'

'Possibly. He always said there were herbs and potions on the island that would have cured her had he thought to bring them, or better still, left her behind.'

'It's awful. Did he never marry again?'

Alex shook his head.

'Grief, rage, guilt, they consumed him for months then, he told me, one night Celeste appeared to him in a dream and told him what he must do. So he went right ahead and did it, in memory of her, he always said . . . hey.'

He suddenly pointed to the horizon.

'Do you see that boat, like a small luxury liner?'

He took out pocket binoculars.

'Alex!'

She hit him on the knee.

'Gordon did what?'

He spoke rapidly, his eyes on the yacht.

'Qualified as an engineer, started a small business in Dumfries, helped by his brother, Donald. He built it up, both worked like devils, and they made a fortune. They bought St Christos, brought their sister over here and proceeded to set the island straight, economically and financially.'

'Crikey,' Tessa said.

'Indeed. A great story.'

'What happened to the other two?'

'His sister, Mabel, returned to Scotland. Couldn't stand the life although she came back to visit frequently before she died thirty years ago. Donald was happy here and he set up house with Bella's sister. He died a few years after Mabel.'

'Did they have children?' Tessa asked, hopeful of a genuine St Christos relative.

'No, otherwise maybe Gordon would have left the island to a child of his brother's.'

'And I wouldn't be here.'

'Probably not.'

The light was fading now, a large shadowy moon putting the sun to flight.

One or two of the town's lights shone below. Alex put his hands on Tessa's shoulders, turning her to face him.

'I'm glad you're here. Whatever happens to St Christos, I'm glad it brought you here.'

He picked up a handful of her hair, now loose and thick around her face.

'The magic's got you, hasn't it, Tessa? You're so different here, and absolutely beautiful.'

'Am I?' she whispered.

His face was so close to hers, the moonlight so persuasive, the kiss was inevitable. First, a soft, light touch and then another until they were pressed together, their kisses slowly deepening into a passionate embrace.

'Tessa?'

Alex lifted his head, looking deep into her eyes. She broke free.

'I . . . I'm sorry,' she said.

'I'm sorry, too.'

He attempted a laugh.

'I told you the island's magic. It has

bewitched our reason. Blame St Christos, and you, Tessa, your beauty bewitched me.'

'I'm not beautiful.'

He frowned and she was suddenly reminded of Jerry.

'Don't undersell yourself. You are lovely and I have to say I envy that handsome guy you're engaged to, and I'd like to throw him over that cliff.'

She was grateful he'd lightened the moment and the silence was friendly as they watched the moon rise, flooding the island with brilliant light. He leaned forward.

'That ship, it's anchored off the island and they're lowering a dinghy. See the lights? Who on earth!'

They were directly above the jetties and could see clearly the figures in the dinghy as the powerful outboard motor raced it up to the main jetty.

'It must be the men in suits.'

He strained to see but briefly a cloud obscured the moon and the figures darkened. Tessa took his binoculars and clutched Alex's arm.

'Oh, good heavens!'

The moon saw off the cloud and re-illuminated the scene below.

'What? What is it?' Alex demanded.

'I do not believe this. It's . . . it's impossible.'

Just then, the figures reached the jetty and looked up. Tessa drew back, pulling Alex with her.

'I know they can't possibly see me,' she hissed, 'but it's Jerry, and my mother!'

9

At the entrance to the lane, Alex stopped and said, 'I won't come any farther, if you're absolutely sure it was your mother and Jerry.'

'I'm sure, but please come in, if only for a few minutes. Something awful might have happened, and they may not even be at the house.'

Tessa held his hand tightly as they went up to the house. Lights cut sharply into the night, figures moved across the windows.

'There's definitely someone there,' Alex said.

'Mother and Jerry, I know it is.'

She took a deep breath and opened the door.

'Darling, Tessa.'

Jerry rushed forward and took her in his arms, kissing her before she could speak. Behind him, Bella registered bewilderment and faint disapproval. Looking for once less than her immaculate self, Margaret got up from a chair and yawned.

'Terrible ride on that tiny plane,' she complained, 'and I hope you can find us a bed for the night.'

'I expect we'll manage something,' Bella said. 'I'll make some coffee, and I don't suppose Alex and Tessa have eaten.'

'No. We saw the boat and came straight back here,' Tessa said. 'We were going to eat at Curtis's brother's fish place.'

She disengaged herself from Jerry's embrace.

'I thought you were too busy to come here with me, Jerry, and you, Mother, why are you here? Weren't you supposed to be somewhere else?'

'I told you. You never listen to me. I was . . . '

'I must go,' Alex said suddenly and moved to the door.

'Not on our account, I hope. I'm

sorry to spoil your evening.'

Jerry clamped his arm round Tessa's waist.

'You didn't, and I have to go,' Alex insisted. 'Tessa, you'll keep in touch? Let me know . . . '

'Of course, and thanks for tonight.'

He nodded and left. Tessa turned to her visitors.

'So why are you here?' she repeated. 'Not that I'm not glad to see you, but both of you are so busy I thought it was impossible.'

'It's not entirely social,' Margaret said, 'and personally I'd no wish to set foot on this island, but, as I was saying, you never remember any of my itineraries. I did mention I was guest speaker in New York on Wednesday, at a fund-raising dinner. Jerry was in Washington. We both needed to speak to you urgently and as you never phoned, and communication with this island appears to be mediaeval, it seemed a good idea to meet up and come together. Tell her your news first, Jerry.'

'What's the news that's so urgent, Jerry?'

'It's all happening so fast. You know I had to go to Washington?'

'Yes.'

'The conference went marvellously well and at the end of it I was offered a job, head of obstetrics and gynaecology at one of America's most prestigious hospitals. It's a teaching hospital and, best of all, it's got one of the best research teams in the world. It's a dream. The woman in charge of research is a professor, one of the brightest and best and one of the youngest professors in the States. Her name's Carole. You'll love her.'

'Will I? But you've got a job in England.'

'Don't be dense, Tessa,' Margaret butted in impatiently. 'This is the opportunity of a lifetime. Jerry couldn't possibly turn it down. He's been head-hunted by the top of his profession and you should be proud of him.'

'Of course I'm pleased for him but

this means you'll be living in Washington?'

'I can hardly commute from London. It's a high-pressure job and of course we'll be living in Washington.'

Bella came in just at that moment with a laden tray.

'Thanks,' Margaret said. 'Put it on the table. We'll help ourselves.'

'I can do that.'

Bella made to pour coffee.

'No, thank you, we're having a private discussion here.'

'Mother!' Tessa cried angrily. 'Bella is . . . '

'It's all right,' Bella interrupted quietly. 'I'll leave you to it. I've made up two beds, one in the study and one in my room. I shall go and stay with my sister and be back to prepare your breakfasts. Good-night.'

'Mother,' Tessa repeated after Bella's dignified exit, 'that wasn't necessary. Bella's not a servant.'

'How was I to know that? I'll have some more coffee then I'll leave you two. I'm quite tired.'

'Tell me how you came to be here.'

'I just told you. I had a date in New York but before I left, Douglas McGuire contacted me with news about St Christos. I phoned Jerry. You were impossible to get hold of and you never phoned so we decided to meet up in Washington and come here together.'

'What news about St Christos?'

'What we expected. It's all clear. You can sell it and best news of all, Toplan have increased their offer. They're very keen. They've surveyed the island, drawn up plans.'

'They had no right to do that,' Tessa exclaimed angrily. 'Who gave them permission? Apparently someone's been snooping around, even planning a heliport.'

'I suppose McGuire gave them the go-ahead,' Jerry said with a frown. 'I don't see the harm in it. We are going to sell the place.'

'I haven't decided that yet.'

Jerry and Margaret looked at her in amazement.

'But that's why you're here, isn't it?' Margaret asked. 'To see for yourself, get an idea what it may be worth.'

'No! That was not my idea. I came to see what Dad found so special about St Christos, and it is unique. I love it here.'

'It's just another tiny Caribbean island surely, nothing special,' Jerry said casually. 'You'd be mad to turn down Toplan's offer.'

'You haven't seen the place,' Tessa exploded. 'How can you tell?'

'We came up through what the man said was the main town. Looked pretty rundown to me. Anyway,' Margaret went on, 'we need you to come back with us. You have to sign some papers. We've a provisional booking in first class for tomorrow night.'

'Tomorrow! I can't. I've a ticket for next Saturday. Jerry was away and Molly told me you were, too, so I extended my visit. I did phone. I don't

148

have to be at work until next Monday.'

'Well, you'll just have to unextend it,' her mother said tartly. 'I really don't know what's got into you, Tessa. Ever since this island business you've been impossible. It's all your father's fault. I should never have married the man. I'm sick of the whole thing. Just show me where I'm to sleep tonight.'

When Tessa came back, Jerry had produced a bottle of champagne from a cool bag.

'From the flight,' he said. 'I found a couple of glasses in the kitchen. Don't take any notice of Margaret. She's had a very busy schedule.'

'Hasn't she always? And she's right, theirs was a doomed marriage from the start. I'm beginning to realise that now.'

He poured out the wine and raised his glass.

'Too late for them even if you are right, so let's concentrate on us and our golden future in America.'

He kissed her but her response was tinged with the guilty memory of Alex's kiss. Jerry either didn't notice or chose to ignore her lack of passion.

'You look well,' he conceded. 'St Christos certainly suits you, and America will, too. It's nearer St Christos if you want to pop over and see how the development goes.'

'Jerry, you don't understand. The sort of development Toplan Leisure would build here would be totally wrong. I would be betraying Gordon and my father. I have obligations to them both.'

'And your obligation to me? Our future? Doesn't that count? Carole was so enthusiastic about my taking the job. She's dying to meet you and help you house-hunt.'

'I'm not sure I want to live in America. I like my job at home,' she said.

'There's a lot of scope for you in the States, and with the money from the sale of this island, you could afford to set up a private clinic.'

'Jerry! You just won't listen to me at all.'

He took her in his arms.

'No, perhaps because I don't want to. I hate to see you so blinkered. St Christos has become an obsession. There's only one issue as far as I can see, one question. Answer truthfully, do you love me, Tessa?'

She blotted out the treacherous memory of Alex's kiss. It had merely been the magic of the moonlight clouding her reason. Of course she loved Jerry and she was so lucky he loved her.

'Yes, I do,' she told him.

'Then there's no problem. We'll be married very soon and you'll quickly forget about this place. You're coming back with us tomorrow.'

'I can't do that. I have to go to a wedding.'

'When is it?'

'In the morning.'

'No problem then. Our flight leaves Barbados at midnight. We'll leave right after the wedding. Whose wedding is it anyway?'

'Just friends of Alex and it's on St Marques.'

'He's going, too?'

'He's a witness, and I promised to be one, too.'

'The boat will take us there. There's an airstrip on St Marques. We came in there this evening. I'll charter a plane in the morning while you pack.'

Tessa nodded, pushing away the feeling she was losing control of her life, again. But what direction did she want to take? Jerry offered a glamorous, exciting life in the States, surely enough for any woman. The alternative was to dig in her heels over St Christos and fulfil her obligation to an unknown great-uncle. She loved the island but maybe it was merely a romantic illusion to believe she could maintain its way of life. There were too many difficulties, with opposition from Jerry and from her mother, and practical logistical problems. It was impossible. With a sigh, she settled for Jerry's kisses and champagne, hoping to blot out the guilt of her betrayal.

★   ★   ★

Jeannie and Mark exchanged vows on the beach at St Marques. It was a simple ceremony with only Alex and Tessa as witnesses. Jeannie, in a plain blue dress, was the most radiant bride Tessa had ever seen and Mark's love for her was apparent in every look and touch. With the ocean a gentle, moving background, they kissed and twined around each other before thanking Tessa and Alex.

'As perfect as I imagined it,' Jeannie said. 'That's always how I wanted it to be. We'll have a party in England for our families but this was just for the two of us.'

She hugged Tessa.

'I hope things turn out OK for you. He's very handsome, your fiancé.'

Jerry had brought her down to the beach and was waiting to drive her to the airfield where Margaret was longing to get back to civilisation. Tessa glanced at Alex as he kissed the bride but he didn't look happy.

'I'm sorry you can't stay for the party, Tessa, and that you're leaving St Christos so suddenly.'

'It has to be. I'm sorry, too. I'll write to you.'

'It would be useful to know your intentions regarding the island,' he said formally. 'Whatever you decide, I wish you luck in the future.'

He linked arms with Jeannie and Mark.

'Let's go. There are a few friends in town waiting.'

He turned away from Tessa and walked up the beach with the bride and groom. Tessa felt as though her world had been snatched from her. With one last look towards St Christos, she walked up the beach to join Jerry and head for London.

London was hot, sticky and thundery. Tessa longed for the ocean-cooling breezes of the Caribbean, and also wished she was back at work. Margaret had presented her with a daunting list of things to be done before the big day.

Jerry himself seemed to have lost interest in the wedding preparations except to contact his scattered family and invite them to London. His main focus of interest had shifted to his future in Washington.

'Just so long as we're married, I really don't care what colour the table decorations are,' he said. 'Hey, have you seen these brochures Carole's sent through? There's a new residential area being developed near the hospital, very expensive, but the ultimate in luxury.'

'Obviously Carole's an old friend now,' Tessa commented somewhat waspishly. 'I'm surprised you don't invite her to the wedding.'

'What an excellent idea,' he said and kissed her. 'We'll do just that.'

The worse pressure came from Douglas McGuire. Every day he rang to urge her to come and sign the contracts with Toplan for the sale of St Christos. Tessa found it impossible to focus on a decision, made every excuse and in the end filtered all calls through Molly. She knew it was cowardly but the thought of Bella reading her farewell letter as they'd left St Christos at dawn, wrung her heart. She had betrayed them all by running back to London and it had made her miserable.

The wedding was a bare two weeks away and she was mercifully back at work, loving her paediatric nursing, but she began to dream about the island. In the dream its beauty was as she remembered but everything had fallen into decay. Bella sat among the ruins of the school as a bulldozer poised to scoop up the rubble. She woke sweating with fear, knowing she could no longer delay her decision.

Jerry was leaving for Washington for a few days to finalise his new contracts. She saw him off at the airport.

'Next time at Heathrow we'll be flying off on honeymoon, to a proper

156

Caribbean island.'

'Sure. I'd better go. Helen and I have a final fitting this afternoon.'

It was probably the fitting that did it. Her dress was still too elaborate for her taste. Helen's was much simpler, elegant and unfussy.

'Kenneth, there's still too much stuff in that train. Cut it right back, and it's so hot, can you make it sleeveless? I really don't like these.'

'But you look lovely,' Helen said, surprised. 'I think it's perfect.'

'Really? I feel so overdressed.'

'It's not your usual style, but maybe you should go in for more glamour.'

'I am not glamorous.'

Tears welled up, her voice shook. Kenneth and Helen looked appalled.

'Hey, calm down. We'll go and have a drink. You're stressed out. Leave the dress as it is,' Helen told Kenneth, 'well, maybe shorten the train.'

They found a cool, dark wine bar and Helen fetched a bottle of chilled Chardonnay from the bar.

'For goodness' sake, drink this and tell me what the problem is.'

Obediently, Tessa drank.

'Liquid sunshine,' she said, 'that's better. Thanks, Helen. I'm sorry.'

'For what? You haven't changed your mind about marrying Jerry?'

'No-oo, it's just, everything's happening so fast. I have to decide about St Christos and this wedding. It's too big, too grand.'

She told Helen about Jeannie's and Mark's beach wedding.

'That's what I'd prefer, and, Helen, I don't really want to live in Washington. Isn't that awful?'

'No. It's a big change, but if you love Jerry . . . '

'I do. At least I think I do, but he and Mother, they're so dismissive about St Christos. It's not important to them except as a cash prize.'

'And you like it? It does sound wonderful.'

'I love it, and I left in such a hurry, never saying goodbye properly to Bella or Alex. Next the bulldozers will move in. Helen, I don't think I can stand it.'

Tears sprang in her eyes again. Helen passed over a tissue.

'In my expert medical opinion, you are suffering from shock and stress. You'll crack up at this rate and there won't be a wedding.'

She thought for a few moments while Tessa mopped her eyes then said slowly, 'Here's an idea. Call it crazy but listen anyway. Can you get time off before the wedding?'

'Yes. I'm still owed a week's leave and Jerry's cut short the honeymoon because of Washington. Why?'

'I can take a few days off. Jerry's away, isn't he?'

'Yes.'

'And your mother?'

'She'll be in Italy, a follow-up seminar arranged months ago. I can't remember exactly but I think she's going on to the States.'

'You're not having a hen party, are you?'

'No, just a few drinks with people at work. What's this leading to?'

'I think your trouble is you didn't have a chance to get St Christos out of your system. It was new and wonderful and you didn't have a chance to see the impracticalities of keeping an island the other side of the world though it would be more convenient from the States. If Jerry's going to be earning megabucks you might need an island retreat.'

'No. It has to be a working island maintained as it was in Gordon's time, self-sufficient, profitable, needing a little modernising, of course. I've thought of all sorts of things.'

'Just a minute, Tessa. You're going to sell it, marry Jerry, have a great future, but you need to let go this dream. What I think is, you and I should have a hen party on St Christos, or a hen holiday. I'd love to see it and I'm sure that would get it out of your system, or am I talking rubbish?'

'Helen, you're a genius. We don't need to tell anyone, just go. I'll book a flight tonight. I'll fax Alex. He can tell Bella. You'll love her, and Jeannie and Mark. What a good friend you are. Let's go and pack right now.'

Looking at her friend's animated face and sparkling eyes without a trace of a tear now, Helen wondered if perhaps it really was such a good idea. It was all rather a muddle. She hoped she hadn't made it worse.

★   ★   ★

Tessa searched for Alex amongst the crowd outside the arrival gates.

'I can't see him, can you?' she asked Helen.

'I've never met him if you mean Alex but there's a guy there holding a placard with your name on it.'

'That's not Alex.'

'It's obviously someone sent to meet you.'

The man held out his hand when Helen signalled to him.

'Matt Davidson, Transisland Airways.

Alex asked me to take you to St Marques. He says sorry. He's . . . er . . . tied up right now. Curtis will meet you at the airport.'

'What's the problem with Alex?' Tessa persisted.

'He'll tell you. I might get it wrong. Follow me, ladies.'

At the St Marques landing area Curtis gave her a warm smile.

'Great to see you back so soon, and with a friend.'

'A last pre-wedding fling.'

Tessa hung on to her seat as the truck-taxi bounced over the potholes.

'Peach and Quiet again tonight. Alex and James will meet you there this evening. They're both pretty busy right now.'

'Is Alex in some sort of trouble?'

Curtis turned to face her.

'Should I stop for a few minutes and let your friend take in the view?'

'Yes, please.'

Helen leaped out of the truck and ran to the edge of the cliff. Tessa stayed with Curtis.

'Tell me about Alex.'

'Nothing important. Just a business problem. The very day you left, a rival school appeared out of nowhere, a mile or so along the coast, with a flash, wooden clubhouse. Must've been flatpack for it went up in a couple of days, fancy boats, special cut-price packages, international TV advertising offering exactly what James and Alex do. Consequently the Ross's trade is beginning to look a bit sick.'

'But they're so popular and very professional.'

'Sure, they can stand up-front competition, especially once the novelty of the new place has worn off but last week two boats were wrecked. Securely moored at night they were, yet next morning the boats were adrift. One ran on to the reef, the other overturned.'

'Tessa, it's fantastic,' Helen's excited face appeared, 'These beaches! I can't wait to be there. I need a swim.'

'Peach and Quiet has a great pool and it's right next to the ocean.'

'Wow, I love it. Wasn't this a great idea?'

'It certainly was. Prodded me into action, too. Curtis, can you set up a meeting at Bella's with the top important guys of St Christos?'

'Sure can.'

He pulled up outside the hotel.

'I hope you've got a decision for us.'

'Yes, I have. I'll tell you all at the meeting.'

The Ross cousins joined them for supper and afterwards they strolled along the beach. James and Helen took to each other at once and within minutes James had arranged to take Helen for a dive the next day.

'You as well, Tessa?'

'No. I must go to St Christos, on business.'

Alex's head shot up.

'Island business?'

'Yes. Curtis is fixing a meeting at Bella's. He'll let you know when it is. You should be there.'

'You've made a decision?'

'Yes, but I can't . . . '

'Of course, keep it for the meeting.'

The other two were well ahead, hardly visible in the fading light.

'When you faxed you were coming back, I was sure you were going to finalise the deal with the developers. They've been here again. I'm glad you have the courage to face the islanders and tell them yourself.'

'At the meeting, you'll know. What about you? Curtis says there's trouble.'

'Just a hitch. We'll survive. No-one's going to wipe us off the map. A guy tried to buy us out earlier in the year, a large offer, more than it's worth.'

'You'll not sell?'

'What? Give up all this? Not a chance. The odd thing is, Curtis is convinced this attempt to get rid of us is connected with St Christos. He's most likely imagining intrigue and conspiracy. He loves mysteries. Come on, forget our worries and let's enjoy the rest of the evening.'

The next morning, Curtis took Tessa

to St Christos. Helen, James and Alex would follow in the evening. Three of the island's elders welcomed her.

'There was a lot of disappointment when you left so suddenly with no word about the future,' Curtis explained.

'I can believe it, but I'm here to put that right.'

'Tomorrow's the earliest I could arrange a meeting.'

'That's OK. I can spend the day with Bella.'

Bella's welcome was much more enthusiastic. She kissed Tessa on both cheeks. Tessa glanced at Curtis.

'I'd like to discuss my plan with Bella today.'

'You're the boss. I look forward to tomorrow.'

The two women went into the house.

'Breakfast's on the deck, strong coffee, your favourite banana bread and there's shrimp chowder,' Bella said.

'You spoil me.'

'I'm glad of the opportunity. Now, tell me your plan.'

As Tessa drew a final line under her vision for St Christos, she turned to Bella.

'So what do you think, Bella? Will it work?'

'It's great. I know Gordon would approve. If you had produced it sooner . . . but there's been such a delay and your sudden departure . . . people are suspicious. You might have lost their trust.'

'I hope that's not so, but I'll have to risk it.'

'It depends how tomorrow's meeting goes. All the rumours about development have unsettled people but we'll see.'

Later in the day, when the others arrived, they swam, drank wine and ate Bella's delicious chicken. The atmosphere was light-hearted and Tessa couldn't remember when she'd last enjoyed a day so much. They sat on the beach and watched the pink-streaked sky darken to a fiery red. James put out a hand to Helen.

'Let's walk down to the water.'

Alex cleared the remains of the barbecue then sat back on his heels and looked at Tessa intently.

'Can you tell me what you've decided about St Christos?'

'I'd rather wait until the meeting. It's only fair.'

'But you're going back to London to be married?'

'You know I am. A week on Saturday.'

'So you're still Tessa Ferguson for eight more days, and this is St Christos not London so I guess I'm entitled . . .'

He took her in his arms and kissed her. Briefly she protested but a deep, passionate hunger swept away her scruples and she kissed him back. The magic of the island engulfed her. London would return her common-sense. It was Alex who broke away first. Still holding her, he touched her hair.

'You should stay here,' he murmured softly. 'Keep the magic.'

'Ssh, you know I can't. I have to be

practical. There's Jerry and . . . '

'All right,' he cut her short, 'I know that. We'll go back now. I've a dawn dive to supervise in the morning.'

'I'm sorry.'

She felt a numbing pain in her heart as she watched him pick up the rugs and towels.

'Don't be. We can always blame the magic of St Christos. Who knows, if you'd come here as a little girl we might have found and kept that magic.'

He kissed her lightly on the cheek.

'Be happy, Tessa. I'll see you at the meeting tomorrow.'

'Alex . . . '

He put a finger to her lips.

'No, don't say any more. Don't make it worse. Let's go.'

★   ★   ★

The old men were getting restless. Harry, the oldest and most respected, finally spoke.

'We will start without Alex and

Curtis. Maybe their boat broke down. There's obviously a delay but we have no more time to waste. Speak to us, Tessa Ferguson. You have kept us in suspense too long.'

'I'm sorry for that. I can only apologise, ask your forgiveness and tell you right away I have no intention of selling St Christos for tourist development.'

There was a murmur of approval or was it surprise? It was hard to tell from the impassive faces of the old men sitting in Bella's living-room.

'I want to carry on my great uncle's design for St Christos. It's all written here,' she went on and tapped a pile of folders. 'A committee will be formed to oversee the workings of the plan, continue to develop the island's resources, expand markets, some modernisation, a clinic, more amenities, a limited amount of tourism but strictly controlled.'

As she spoke Bella handed out the folders.

'There should be more jobs, keep the young people.'

She stopped. They had ceased to listen as the old men turned into a kindergarten of excited youngsters leafing through the folders and talking among themselves in a dialect Tessa didn't understand.

'I think they like it and I think you've . . . ' Bella began, then broke off.

'Here's Curtis, on his own. Something's wrong.'

Tessa followed Bella out to the drive where Curtis leaped from his truck.

'There been an accident on the dive. Alex and James are both hurt.'

'Come back into the house, Tessa,' Bella said.

'No, I have to go to St Marques. Curtis, please, what happened?'

'Alex and James were attacked underwater. The police are there and . . . '

'The police? What happened? How bad is it?'

'I'm afraid Alex is pretty bad. They're flying him to hospital in Barbados. They think they can patch up James on St Marques.'

Terror welled in Tessa's heart. She felt dizzy, breathless. If anything happened to Alex . . .

'I must see him. Take me back with you, please, Curtis.'

'But the meeting?' Bella queried.

'The main part's over. You can carry on. Take a note of the opinions. You know, everything we talked about yesterday. Curtis, can we go now?'

'He may already be on his way to Barbados. They were trying to rustle up an emergency plane. He's lost a lot of blood. He was stabbed.'

She buried her head in her hands as she got into the truck and they roared off. Curtis picked up his story.

'All I know is it was on an early-morning dive. Both Alex and James were attacked and the clients panicked. But you mustn't worry. Everything will be OK. Now, tell me about the meeting. That may take your mind off things.'

They reached St Marques just in time to see the plane soar into the blue sky towards Barbados and Tessa watched it with a dreadful sense of doom. She wanted to catch the next Transisland plane and follow it, but when Helen telephoned the school from St Christos, she dissuaded her.

'It wouldn't do any good, especially as Alex is unconscious. In any case, we're in Barbados tomorrow for our flight home. Either come back now or I'll pack your things and bring them over.'

'Helen, I can't go back to London tomorrow.'

'Why not? You've sorted out the St Christos business and there's nothing you can do for Alex. Tessa, you're marrying Jerry next Saturday. We've had a great time here but your island love affair is over.'

In the end, Tessa went back to St Christos to say goodbye to Bella and although she was worried about Alex, for Helen's and Bella's sake, she tried to enjoy the last hours on the island.

'I don't worry any more,' Bella told Tessa just before they left next morning. 'You will be back many times. You are tied to us now, and Alex Ross will be here. Trust me.'

Tessa knew Bella would be part of her life for ever, as would St Christos, whether she lived in Washington or London. Now all her anxiety was for Alex. She and Helen caught the early plane to give them time to visit him in hospital. He was in a private ward, and she tried not to cry out when she saw him, white and still, attached to drips and monitors.

'How bad?' she asked the doctor.

'As you see, he's still unconscious. He's lost a lot of blood but the knife missed his heart by a fraction. Are you a relative?'

'No, just a friend. He will be all right?'

'Hard to tell. We'll know more when he regains consciousness.'

Tessa couldn't leave the bedside.

Time lost meaning. Helen brought her juice, coffee, a sandwich which she couldn't eat, and finally she said, 'Tessa, we must go. The plane leaves in an hour.'

'I'm not going, not until I've spoken to Alex.'

'What for? He may be out for days. You can write, phone, e-mail. You have to get back for Saturday. We'll miss that plane unless we go now.'

'I'm not coming.'

'Tessa,' Helen cried out in exasperation but as she watched Tessa watching Alex, she realised it was pointless.

'I will be there Saturday. I'll telephone. They'll understand.'

Helen hugged her friend, gave a thumbs-up sign for luck to the unconscious Alex and left for the airport. Halfway across the Atlantic, half-dozing, half-dreaming, she wondered if Kenneth could alter her bridesmaid dress to be suitable for casual evening wear!

Tessa took a room at a small hotel

near the hospital. Part of the day she spent talking to Bella on the newly-installed telephone at Gordon's house. Everyone was delighted with her proposal and work had already started in the fields. Fishing boats were busy again and applications for discreet guest house development were trickling in.

The rest of the day she spent sitting by Alex's side, willing him back to consciousness, talking to him quietly about her plans for St Christos, hoping to rouse him from his coma.

On the second day of her vigil Curtis joined her.

'I can see there's no change,' he said gloomily.

'He'll be OK. He hasn't told me what he thinks of my plan yet.'

Curtis was non-committal.

'What I do know now is who was behind all this and why. At first we guessed it was just another company wanting to muscle in. That would have been fair enough but these guys had been specially hired to smash the Ross business by fair means or foul, though I doubt they meant to go this far.'

'But why?'

'St Christos is why. Of course we can't prove a thing. After the accident the guys along the coast left in a hurry. Gear gone, premises abandoned. I've traced a link to the Toplan Leisure Company and to the lawyer, McGuire. They wanted to get their hands on St Christos and to develop St Marques as a top-class, water-sport resort. They were sure you'd sell and if they could get hold of the Ross establishment and land they'd be made. Seems your fiancé told them he could easily persuade you so they moved in, a mite too hasty as it turned out.'

'Jerry was in on this?'

'I wouldn't go that far but my informants tell me there were some secret meetings on St Christos with a few disaffected locals and the men in the white suits. Whether he was there with them or not, I can't say.'

'Jerry may have his faults but he's not

. . . can't be a saboteur.'

'Well, that's for you to deal with. I have to say from the atmosphere on St Christos you've certainly cracked that one.'

If only my own problem was as easy, Tessa thought as she focused once more on Alex.

Later, when she got back to her hotel room, the phone was ringing.

'Tessa,' a voice said in her ear, and her spirits took a dive.

'Mother, er, nice to hear you. You got my fax about St Christos?'

'I did and I'm not interested. You'll return immediately. Why did you go back there without a word to anyone? However, you can still sign the sale contract. Mr McGuire has been very patient.'

'I'm not selling.'

'That place has addled your brain. The wedding is four days away.'

'How is Jerry?'

'He's in Washington.'

'Washington? What's he doing there?'

'Some woman, Catherine, or Carole, keeps inventing excuses to keep him there. You'll lose him if you don't act at once. Hasn't he been in touch?'

'No, not a word.'

The silence was prolonged then came the explosion.

'If you're not on the next plane, Tessa, that's it! I'm through with you. You and your blasted island!'

'I will be there for Saturday. I promised, didn't I?'

'For goodness' sake! All right then, don't bother, because I don't think Jerry's interested any more. Given half a chance, this Caroline woman will sink her claws in him and I think Jerry might have finally met his match. You know he never really loved you. He told me you were different, self-contained. He admired you and I'm sure he wanted you. I could never see why but he thought he could mould you to his requirements.'

'Mother, don't say any more. I want to stay friends with you. Don't make it impossible.'

She put the receiver down and went back to the hospital, but before she left, she put through a call to the hotel where Jerry had previously stayed in Washington . . .

It was late Friday before Alex showed any signs of life. Tessa had dozed off when the nurse checking him said, 'He's stirring. Take his hand, Tessa.'

She took it in both of hers and squeezed gently. His eyelids flickered, opened, closed, opened again, focusing in disbelief.

'Tessa?'

'I'm here,' she said, 'and I'm never going away.'

He sighed, turned his head and slept peacefully.

* * *

How strange, Tessa thought, as she yawned and stretched on the hospital cot, it's my wedding day. A nurse came in with a cup of tea.

'Are you OK? You were so exhausted last night.'

'I'm fine, and thanks. I was too tired to make the hotel. How is Alex?'

'Awake, and says he dreamed of this girl who's about to be married.'

'Yes, it is today but I'm not, nor is Jerry. I've talked to him. I know now it would have been like marrying my mother. He admitted it, too. Anyway, this Carole in Washington sounds just like my mother, so they'll be very happy.'

She beamed and sipped her tea.

'Don't worry, I'm fine, just deliriously happy. Can I go see Alex?'

'I think you'd better. I just hope he can take it.'

'We can get married on the beach now, our secret beach. I'm sure Bella won't mind.'

'Why don't you just tell him all this?'

'I'm going to, right now.'

Alex was struggling to sit up when she appeared.

'Tessa, it is you. I heard your voice

but I thought it was part of a dream.'

'It was no dream. I'm here, have been all the time. Alex, there's so much to tell you. St Christos, your accident, Jerry and me . . . '

'It's your wedding day,' he interrupted. 'That's what I dreamed, but it can't be because you're here.'

She went to his bedside and put her hand on his.

'It is my wedding day but I'm not marrying Jerry. We had a long talk last night and both realised it would have been a dreadful mistake. We were both marrying for the wrong reasons. Besides, I don't love him. It's you I love and wherever you are I want to be — St Marques, St Christos, even London.'

He took her in his arms.

'Forget London for now. I love you so much, Tessa, and I have done since I first met you in London. We'll marry on Bella's beach as soon as possible. We've wasted time already. Say you will.'

'Of course I will.'

As they embraced, mutual passion swept them away and they knew their future would always hold its own magic on whichever island they found themselves.

THE END

We do hope that you have enjoyed reading this large print book.

Did you know that all of our titles are available for purchase?

We publish a wide range of high quality large print books including:
Romances, Mysteries, Classics
General Fiction
Non Fiction and Westerns

Special interest titles available in large print are:
The Little Oxford Dictionary
Music Book, Song Book
Hymn Book, Service Book

Also available from us courtesy of Oxford University Press:
Young Readers' Dictionary
(large print edition)
Young Readers' Thesaurus
(large print edition)

For further information or a free brochure, please contact us at:
Ulverscroft Large Print Books Ltd.,
The Green, Bradgate Road, Anstey,
Leicester, LE7 7FU, England.
Tel: (00 44) **0116 236 4325**
Fax: (00 44) **0116 234 0205**

VISIONS OF THE HEART

Christine Briscomb

When property developer Connor Grant contracted Natalie Jensen to landscape the grounds of his large country house near Ashley in South Australia, she was ecstatic. But then she discovered he was acquiring — and ripping apart — great swathes of the town. Her own mother's house and the hall where the drama group met were two of his targets. Natalie was desperate to stop Connor's plans — but she also had to fight the powerful attraction flowing between them.

FINGALA, MAID OF RATHAY

Mary Cummins

On his deathbed, Sir James Montgomery of Rathay asks his daughter, Fingala, to swear that she will not honour her marriage contract until her brother Patrick, the new heir, returns from serving the King. Patrick must marry. Rathay must not be left without a mistress. But Patrick has fallen in love with the Lady Catherine Gordon whom the King, James IV, has given in marriage to the young man who claims to be Richard of York, one of the princes in the Tower.